The Co-Parent Project

by

Sandra Dailey

This is a work of fiction. Names, characters, places, and incidents are either the product of the author's imagination or are used fictitiously, and any resemblance to actual persons living or dead, business establishments, events, or locales, is entirely coincidental.

The Co-Parent Project

COPYRIGHT © 2019 by Sandra Dailey

Cover Art by *Debbie Taylor*

The Wild Rose Press, Inc.
PO Box 708
Adams Basin, NY 14410-0708
Visit us at www.thewildrosepress.com

Publishing History
First Crimson Edition, 2019
Print ISBN 978-1-5092-2530-9
Digital ISBN 978-1-5092-2531-6

Published in the United States of America

Dedication

This one is for my twin sister and best friend
Gail Beith.
She's worked tirelessly to brainstorm,
pre-edit, encourage, and keep me on task.
I hope to return the favor soon.

Chapter One

Wednesday, August 1—The Crash

"Are you sure your father knows what he's talking about?" Melissa Wolff asked. "I've never heard of anyone getting a quickie divorce in Mexico."

"If anyone would know about quickie divorces, it would be my dad. He's been married five times." David Wolff was glad for a break from the stupid argument they'd had earlier, but he knew another one would start at any moment.

He tapped a gauge on the control panel of the small private plane. The fuel tank had been filled prior to takeoff. Now, the needle dropped before his disbelieving eyes. What the hell was happening?

Concern snaked through his gut. He couldn't let Melissa know he was worried. She'd go crazy.

"It always comes down to the almighty dollar, doesn't it?" she remarked.

"I've promised you a generous settlement. You can stop complaining any time. Why don't you have another drink?" Alcohol was always her go-to whenever an argument wasn't going her way.

"At least it's cheaper than high-priced hookers, so you can stop complaining as well."

What had happened to their perfect fairytale story?

When had their lives come to this? "It's getting late. How long does it take to get there?"

"I think we may be in trouble. Be quiet."

It wasn't a malfunctioning gauge. The engines were starting to sputter. They were losing power. Outside the window, he saw fluid spray from beneath the wing. Fuel was pouring out over the Gulf of Mexico. There was no time to turn back.

David turned the radio dial to the emergency frequency, 121.5, and spoke into his headset. "Mayday! Mayday! Mayday! Can anyone hear me? This is Alpha-239-November, Cessna150. I'm losing fuel. My attitude has dropped to 1200 feet. Last known position thirty miles west of Tampa. Two persons on board. Please respond. Altitude is now 900. Mayday! Mayday! Mayday!"

A few garbled words could be heard through the static, but he couldn't decipher what they were saying.

"What's going on, David? You're scaring me. Is this supposed to be a joke?"

"I'm sorry, Melissa." Their situation was hopeless. David released his right hand from the yoke, and for the first time in years, took her hand. "There's no more time. We're going down."

Rather than watch the surface of the water rush toward them, they stared into each other's eyes with fear and regret. They each whispered the same last word.

"Eric!"

Chapter Two

Thursday, August 2—The Notifications

Luca Wolff rubbed the sleep from his eyes as he walked through the entrance hall to the front door. Someone had rung the bell twice now. As it was eight o'clock in the morning, his father and brother were probably having coffee in the breakfast room. Neither would get off their butts. They didn't accept visitors before nine, and the staff knew better than admit anyone before that time.

He hated this house. It was as large as a palace, as garish as a Las Vegas casino. The wallpaper was too busy, the furniture too spindly, the artwork too large, and the floors too cold and hard. There were at least a dozen statuettes or busts in every room. They broke easily but still seemed to multiply on their own. Break one—three more took its place. It had been hell growing up here as a healthy, active kid.

Whoever was at the door rang for the third time. They'd better have a good reason. Luca had been up working until three. It didn't matter to him that he only wore sleep pants and beard scruff. They'd better not want to sell anything.

Two men stood at the door, one wearing a worn gray suit and the other in an elaborate blue uniform.

According to a recent article in the local newspaper, the second man was the chief of police for Jacksonville, Florida, George Stanford. Each held out badges when he opened the door. The first identified himself as a detective named Mark Anderson. This couldn't be good.

"Can I help you?"

"I'm a personal friend of Mr. Wolff." The chief folded his arms and glared. "I'd like to speak to him if he's home."

Luca wondered if he was supposed to be impressed. A lot of people claimed to be personal friends with his family. He came close to grinning as he realized the police chief probably thought he was a member of the staff.

"Which Mr. Wolff would that be?" Luca covered his mouth with a fist and yawned. "Do you mean Gerald, my father, or Daniel, my brother? I don't recall your name on my own Christmas card list."

"We need to speak to all of you about a serious matter," the older man groused.

"What for? Did someone die?"

The detective looked down and shifted his feet. Luca instantly regretted the stupid remark. His stomach twisted with dread.

The chief's face hardened. "Could you let the others know we're here?"

"Of course, gentlemen. Please come inside." He led them through the entry and down a short hallway until they reached the breakfast room. "Can I get you some coffee?"

Gerald Wolff, the eighty-three-year-old patriarch of the family, sat at the head of the table with a blank expression on his face. His white hair was neatly combed despite the fact he still wore a pair of lightweight pajamas with a plaid cotton robe and slippers. At his right, his eldest son and Luca's sixty-year-old brother, Daniel, looked like a slightly younger version of the old man. Both were short and heavy with small gray eyes and a bottom lip that protruded as though they were pouting. Together, they were the heads of Wolff Enterprises. The unofficial company motto—Seek and Destroy—gave them full rein to squash small businesses and add them to the corporate pie.

"George, what brings you here at this hour?" Gerald indicated the seat to his left for his friend. The detective wasn't a friend and, therefore, was ignored. "Luca, bring George a cup of coffee."

Had he not just offered? Luca poured three cups and placed two at the opposite end of the table for himself and the other odd man out. The detective smiled and nodded his appreciation.

"Gerald, there's no easy way to say this. I came to bring terrible news." The chief redirected his attention to Daniel. "First let me ask you, Daniel, do you still own that small private plane?"

"I do. My son, David, and his wife have taken it to Mexico for a few days."

"I'm afraid they didn't make it. The plane went down about forty miles from the coastline early last night."

The spoon in Daniel's hand clattered onto his saucer. "That's impossible. My son is a well-trained, qualified pilot, and the plane was in perfect condition. I saw them off myself, yesterday afternoon. What do they think was the cause of this accident?"

"We don't know yet." The chief stirred cream into his coffee. "A fishing boat somehow intercepted David's mayday call. He said he was losing fuel. The boat's radio didn't have the power to respond, but luckily, it was able to call the Coast Guard. The debris area was found before it had a chance to disappear under the water fully."

Daniel reached across the table to grab Stanford's coat sleeve. "My son. Where is he?"

"I'm sorry to say there were no survivors." The chief pulled his arm from Daniel's grip. "Both bodies were successfully recovered. They're being held in Tampa pending identification. The cause of death seems clear. It'll be up to the investigators there, but I wouldn't think an autopsy would be needed. It was a tragic accident."

No survivors.

Luca had made it through five tours of duty in the Middle East as a marine and had never heard that phrase until now. Now, it pertained to the best friend he'd had growing up. He and David, actually his biological nephew, were the same age. David had been the only one in the family who hadn't considered him an accident or an embarrassment. They'd practically grown up as twins. They'd attended high school and two years of college together. After which, while David continued in college, Luca chose military duty. The wound caused by their separation never healed. By the time he returned from active service, David had become one of *them*, the third head of the corporate snake known as Wolff Enterprises. Luca still missed the friend David had once been.

"Bullshit!" Gerald suddenly bellowed. "This was no accident. The plane was sabotaged."

Detective Anderson sat the delicate cup back onto its saucer. "What makes you say that, Mister Wolff?"

Gerald pointed an arthritic finger at Luca. "My son is staying here because his house on Crescent Beach was recently blown up. Now, this." He punctuated each word by pounding his fist on the table. "Someone is out to destroy us."

"Father," Luca said in a sedate tone, "the fire department determined that I had a gas leak under the house. It was an accident. Please calm down." He turned to the detective who was scribbling on a notepad. "Thankfully, my staff and I were all out of the house. The only one injured was my handyman, Arnold. He was outside trimming shrubs at the time of the explosion."

"And his last name?" the detective asked with his pen posed over his notepad.

"Campbell." Luca spelled it out. "He's convalescing with his parents in Charleston, North Carolina, right now."

"Bullshit, I say!" Gerald's face had turned an angry shade of red. His father didn't like being dismissed. "I don't believe in coincidences. If my great-grandson wasn't serving a sentence in the juvenile detention center, I'd say he was responsible for both incidents."

"That's ridiculous, Father." Luca stood to pace. "Eric has never been to my house and has no reason to do any of us harm."

"He doesn't need a reason," Gerald snarled. "His mother ruined that boy. God as my witness, he's better off without her."

"Are you saying this boy, currently in the juvenile center, is the son of David and Melissa Wolff?" The detective's brows raised in surprise. "He'll need to be notified as well."

"I'll take care of that." Daniel's voice dripped with scorn. "He is my grandson."

The detective nodded once and continued his inquiry. "Did Mrs. Wolff have any close relatives we'll need to contact?"

"No one who's worth a damn," Gerald blurted.

"Father, show some compassion." Luca turned to Anderson and said, "She had a sister who may still be living in Summer Springs. That's about thirty miles south of Jacksonville. Unless she married, her name would be Sullivan. I think her first name was Joy...it could be short for Joyce...I don't know."

"Find out where she is and send someone out to talk to her," the chief ordered his subordinate. "We've disturbed enough of your morning. I know you have a lot to process and arrangements to make." After shaking Gerald's hand, the chief nodded at Luca and his brother and turned to leave.

Luca walked them to the door. Before Detective Anderson followed his boss out to the car, he handed Luca a business card. "I have a hinky feeling that something is going on here. Call if you need me."

Luca turned the card over in his fingers. He wondered how well the detective's intuition ran.

****

Joy Sullivan had finished her morning appointments and sat at her small kitchen table to enjoy a cheese sandwich and tea while she read the news on her laptop.

The first article, about a private plane that crashed in the Gulf of Mexico, described the mayday call which was heard by a nearby fishing boat. It mentioned the Coast Guard's involvement and that the couple lost in the accident were from Jacksonville. Their names had been withheld pending notification of their families.

How tragic, she thought. Someone close would feel the worst devastation they'd ever known.

When her mother had died three years ago, Joy's world changed. She no longer had someone to share her evenings. However, her mother's long illness had somewhat prepared her for the event. She was glad her mother no longer suffered from the brain tumor that had made her last days a living hell. Pain and morphine reduced the petite woman to the size of a child. Hopefully, the people in the plane hadn't suffered.

A knock sounded on the front door. Joy jumped up and wiped her mouth with a paper towel. The supplies she'd ordered for her hair salon were scheduled to arrive today.

Instead of a man wearing a brown shirt and shorts, she found a plainclothes police officer. His badge was clipped to his belt. Understandably, he wasn't wearing a jacket in the afternoon heat. "My name is Detective Mark Anderson. Are you Miss Joy Sullivan?"

"Yes, sir. What can I do for you?"

The identification card showed he was from the Jacksonville Police Department...but this wasn't Jacksonville.

"I'd like to come inside and speak to you for a moment, if I may."

"What is this about?" she asked as she stepped back to let him in.

"Ma'am, I'm here to speak to you about your sister and her husband."

****

Joy didn't realize her brain had subconsciously made the connection until she woke up on her lumpy living room sofa. The detective was leaning over her, patting her cheek and offering her a glass of water.

Joy slowly rose to a sitting position. She was utterly alone now. The realization hit her like a punch to her stomach. There'd be no more monthly visits from her only sister and closest friend. Giggling as she trimmed Melissa's hair or walking into town to have lunch at the Summer Springs Café were now history. Ice cream cones as they sat on a bench in the town square were a thing of the past. They'd never again share ideas regarding makeup shades or hem lengths.

"How did they die?" she croaked.

"Quickly. Painlessly. They'd lost consciousness before it happened."

Thank God he understood what concerned her most.

"Where is Eric? Is he okay?"

"His grandfather is taking care of him. You should hear from him soon."

Not likely.

Joy hadn't seen nor heard from Eric in three years, not since her mother's funeral. The Wolffs had put their collective foot down about contact between her nephew and herself.

According to them, she was a disgrace with no culture or class. Her only achievements were a high school diploma and beauty school certificate. Her only assets were a nineteen-fifties, bungalow-style house in a small suburban town and the attached, single-car garage which she'd converted into a small hair salon. Worst of all, she had been born under a veil of scandal. They didn't want her name connected to theirs.

"I'm sure the Wolff family will be in touch as soon as your sister and brother-in-law have been returned and arrangements are made."

"Thank you." There was no need to explain. "You've been very kind."

Chapter Three

Monday, August 6—The Lawyers

Barbara Allgood rearranged strands of hair Joy had carefully styled moments earlier. At times like this, Joy wondered why people paid for the work, then mussed with it. Thankfully, Barbara was the last customer of the day.

"I still can't believe you're related to the Wolffs," Barbara said as she continued to fuss and fiddle. "They're by far the wealthiest family in the county, maybe the state. I'd bet that funeral is going to be the biggest blowout of the year.

Tears loomed behind Joy's eyes; a huge lump clogged her throat every time she thought about her sister's death. Emotions seemed to crop up at odd times every day. Especially with certain customers. Sundays became her only reprieve. It would be nice to take a little time off, but she had bills to pay. This particular job would be easier if Barbara weren't the most insensitive person in all of Summer Springs, Florida. But she was also a regular paying client. Not many women in this little town could afford weekly visits.

"I'm not related to the Wolffs," she said. "My sister married into the family. The only time I've been in the same room with them was during her wedding. I can't tell you a single thing about them. As far as the funeral goes, I haven't heard a word about it yet."

"Hmmm, I bet it'll be this weekend. That would be more convenient for all the people expected to fly in from all over the country. I don't suppose you could arrange an invite for me."

Barbara made the double funeral sound like Prince Charming's royal ball. There wouldn't be a happily-ever-after ending to this occasion.

"To be honest, Barbara, I'll be lucky if I'm allowed to go."

"They aren't hung up on that issue about your background, are they? Things like that are common these days, especially among the lower class." Barb winced. "Sorry, I forgot your family was in the country-club set when all that came down."

Barbara was frank and inappropriate by nature, but Joy knew she meant no harm. "I can't think about that now. I'm too nervous about an appointment with the Wolff's lawyer this evening."

"What kind of appointment?"

"I don't know. The attorney said it was regarding something in my sister's will."

"Ohhh." Barbara rubbed her hands together like a silent movie villain. "I love wills—especially when they involve rich people. You should have told me sooner. I am an attorney, you know. I can go with you and make sure you aren't taken advantage of. I'll even drive, so you don't have to pay cab fare."

Joy planned to take the bus and hoped the meeting would be over before they stopped running. "I can't afford an attorney, Barbara."

"It'll be pro bono, kid. I'd do anything to get in on

13

a little Wolff family drama. Don't worry; I'll be perfectly professional and discreet. You've never seen me in the courtroom. Cross my heart, I turn into a consummate professional."

Joy was aware Barbara was an attorney, but she had no idea what kind of law she practiced. They had both attended the same high school in Summer Springs, but Barbara was several years ahead of Joy. After college and a short marriage, Barbara returned to her hometown and hung out her shingle.

Barbara had been thrilled to find out Joy had opened a hair salon in the neighborhood. She'd become a loyal client but not a real friend. She enjoyed places featuring loud music and strong drinks while Joy was a stay-at-home girl who appreciated good books. Still, it was fun to hear her talk about her wild adventures in the city.

"This is just an informal meeting."

"Sure, it is," she replied dryly. "How many times has that happened? Honey, if they want to talk to you, they definitely have something up their sleeves. Taking your own attorney would keep them in their proper place."

Barbara was right. Maybe she did need someone on her side. Attorneys didn't show up at her door offering free help every day.

****

Luca sat in his lawyer's conference room, annoyed. Something seemed a little too slick about Michael Knight—or his annoyance could be his own prejudice. He didn't trust anyone who did business with his family. However, Knight had called this meeting saying he needed to discuss a will he'd drawn up for David.

His arrogant voice had set Luca's nerves on edge.

Instead of being directed to the attorney's office, he'd been led to this large room. It was void of any personality. Glass windows covered by closed blinds faced the hallway. Large bare windows looked out on the sun halfway sitting behind the Jacksonville skyline. The sunset was beautiful, but it reminded him the day was nearly over and he hadn't had a bite to eat since breakfast.

There was a long black cabinet at one end of the room that held a pitcher of ice water, now already dripping with condensation, and four small glasses. Was that the best they could do?

At the other end of the room low black shelves held a set of legal books—the current year printed boldly on the spines of each one. On top were copies of legal journals, note pads, and pens.

The table running down the center of the room was also black with eight cushioned chairs on each side and one at each end. The chairs were a darker shade of gray than the walls, but matched the carpeting perfectly. It was like waking up to find yourself in an old black-and-white movie. They needed a new decorator.

Attorney Knight finally walked in, file folder in his hand and an air of confidence in his step. He should be confident. His Italian suit was hand stitched, which doubled its value. "I'm glad you could make it on such short notice, Luca."

They'd never met before. They were not friends—and never would be. He wasn't into elitism, like his father, but a certain amount of protocol should be practiced here, beginning with *not* addressing a client he'd never met by his first name.

"What is this about, Knight?"

"If you could hang on just a moment longer," the lawyer said as a tap sounded on the door. "There she is now."

"She who?"

When the door opened, he knew Joy Sullivan right away. He rose as she walked in the room. The woman was as beautiful now as she'd been the one time he saw her at David's wedding. Fifteen years changed her from a soft blossom to an exotic orchid.

Her wild, dark gold curls were longer and fuller now, and held back with a silk scarf. A touch of makeup highlighted stunning green eyes. She had skin the color of melted caramel. The only jewelry she wore was a pair of gold chandelier earrings and a black ribbon choker. Her white peasant blouse had been embroidered with colorful flowers across the top, and a ruffled, black skirt covered her legs to mid-calf. She didn't seem at all aware of her gypsy-like sex appeal. As far as he was concerned, no man could resist that.

"Good evening, Mr. Knight." She held out a hand. "I hope you don't mind that I brought a friend."

That's when Luca noticed the large build, brassy redhead behind Joy. He figured she was either a lawyer or a professional wrestler. He'd stick with lawyer, considering the severe navy suit and matching pumps she was wearing.

"My name is Barbara Allgood; I'm an attorney, here to represent Miss Sullivan."

"That's really not necessary," Knight said as he let go of Joy's hand.

Allgood turned to her client. "When those words are spoken, it usually means you're about to get screwed."

"Come in, Ms. Allgood," Luca corrected as he offered his hand to the older woman. "It's not a problem at all. I'm Luca Wolff."

Joy's direct green gaze tickled his senses. "Do you know what's going on here, Mr. Wolff?"

"Not a clue, but please, have a seat." He turned to Knight. "These ladies have come all this way, and it's getting late. Can we get to the point of this meeting?"

"Certainly." Michael directed the ladies to sit at one side of the long black table before he and Luca sat across from them. He folded his hands to cover the folder in front of him. "It has become necessary for me to reveal part of David and Melissa's wills before the actual reading. There seems to be a conflict between the wills."

"What kind of conflict?" Barbara asked.

He continued as though her presence was of no importance. "I can't show you the wills until the formal reading after the funerals."

"When will that be?" Joy interrupted.

Luca was tired of waiting to get on the topic of discussion, but he couldn't fault Joy when her brows puckered, probably from anxiety of not knowing what was going on. He noticed she was rubbing goose bumps that covered her bare arms. Was the air conditioner set at a level for the comfort of the men in suits, or to cause discomfort for the lesser dressed women? He'd seen his father plan such things at meetings he'd attended at Wolff Enterprises.

"I don't have that information yet, but I'm afraid this subject can't wait." Attorney Knight changed position. Luca figured it was for dramatic effect—or to indicate the time for interruptions was over. "Besides a few small bequests to charities and staff, Mr. David Wolff left seventy-five percent of his wealth to his son, Eric. The money will be held in trust for him until the age of twenty-five. You, Luca, will be the executor of that trust. Also, he left you the remaining twenty-five percent and named you Eric's guardian if he died before Eric reached majority, which is what has happened."

"Why do I need to be here for this, Mr. Knight?" Joy asked.

"I agree," Luca stated. "It seems fairly cut-and-dried to me."

"It was," Michael agreed, "until we read Mrs. Wolff's will. Melissa was quite successful with the stock market. She has left it all to you, Miss Sullivan, and it almost equals the amount Luca will inherit from David. She felt that Eric would always be financially secure due to his father's family."

Knight leaned closer, as though to earn Joy's trust. "Here's the rub, she named you as Eric's guardian." He let that sink into everyone's mind for a few seconds. "This is what I can offer you, Miss Sullivan. The Wolffs will allow you to keep the money Melissa wanted you to have—if you'll give up your claim to your nephew."

"What do you mean, they'll *allow* her to keep the money?" Barbara blurted. "Her sister bequeathed it to her. They have no right to allow anything."

"The family could take her to court on behalf of Eric, claiming the money should be his. They'd have a good chance of winning." Knight opened the folder he'd brought into the room. "Miss Sullivan, I have the forms for you to sign, giving up any claim to Eric. Once that's done, I can write you a check for the amount of your sister's estate." He then took a pen from his inside jacket pocket and offered it to Joy.

Barbara brushed the pen aside. "How much money are we talking about?"

"It doesn't matter." Joy's eyes filled with tears. She rolled her chair back and stood, still gripping the edge of the table. "I won't do it. They can keep the money, but I won't give Eric up. They've kept him away from me for three years. Melissa is gone. He's all I have left."

"Don't be ridiculous," Barbara scolded. She clamped a hand around Joy's wrist to keep her from leaving. "They'll keep your money and still fight you for Eric. We'll take this to court. I'll help you."

"Ask your friend how much she'll charge you for her help, now that she knows you have an inheritance," Knight suggested. "At least fifty percent of the money your sister left you would be my guess. She doesn't have experience with this kind of thing. I'm in courthouses every day, local and federal, and I've never seen her before tonight. If Ms. Allgood had any courtroom experience, I'd know her."

"I'll make the Wolffs pay my fees." Barbara let go of Joy's wrist and faced Knight with a sneer. "Don't try to confuse my client and turn her against me. You'll be seeing plenty of me from now on."

Luca reached across the table to take Joy's hand. He wished they could hash this out privately. "Miss Sullivan, Joy, I would be a good guardian for Eric. I have the means and knowledge needed to guide him in the lifestyle he's used to. Also, I'm strong enough to handle a boy like him."

Confusion was evident in Joy's expression. "What do you mean, *a boy like him*?"

Luca spoke gently as he stood and circled the table to her side. "Eric is currently incarcerated in juvenile detention for stealing a car. He's been in a certain amount of trouble—theft, alcohol use, and vandalism. You've missed quite a bit in the last few years, Ms. Sullivan. It's going to take someone strong to straighten him out."

"Have you ever thought, Mr. Wolff, his lifestyle may be what has led him to act out?" A tear escaped down her cheek. She angrily whisked it away. "I can give him love. According to Melissa, it's a commodity the Wolff family knows nothing about. I'm not going to give him up." She turned to stare directly at Michael Knight. "Sir, you can take those papers and shove them where the sun doesn't shine."

The men watched Barbara Allgood follow Joy out of the room before Luca turned on the lawyer. "What the hell was that? You totally blindsided me with this information. Who authorized you to make her that offer?"

Knight calmly replaced his pen into his pocket and closed the folder. "After I informed your father and brother of the situation, they suggested it. They were sure you'd be agreeable."

"This situation, as you call it, is between Miss Sullivan and me. If you want to represent me, it will stay that way. Is that understood? Leave my father and brother out of it. I fight my own battles. Get on board with that or get lost."

"If you say so, Luca."

Luca bared his teeth and growled like an actual wolf. When he stormed from the room, he slammed the door behind him and heard its glass panel crack. This ass-hat was still not his friend.

Chapter Four

Monday, August 6—Home Sweet Home

Joy regretted storming out of the lawyer's office the way she had. She must have looked like a low-class, out-of-control fishwife. Did she really make that rude comment to Luca Wolff's shyster lawyer? She'd never done such a thing before, but he'd made her so angry. Why did people like the Wolffs think they were superior? To be fair, she admitted Luca Wolff had been pleasant. He seemed to be as surprised by Mr. Knight's statements as she'd been. Maybe that was only an act. People like him learned how to schmooze at an early age. Which brought her back to Eric. What was he like now?

"You haven't heard a word I've said," Barbara complained with a nudge.

The screech of breaks and a car horn sounded as they careened around a corner onto the main road. The inside of Barbara's small economy car replaced the vision of the conference room in her mind. She was right. Joy hadn't heard a single word since they'd left the parking garage.

"I'm sorry. I must have gotten caught up in the scenery. I don't get to Jacksonville often. What did you say?" The city's fancy hotels and high-end restaurants changed to fast-food chains and stop-and-go gas stations the farther they moved into the suburbs.

"I said—the Wolffs will probably look for ways to discredit you. Have you ever been arrested?"

"Certainly not!"

"Have the police ever been called to your house for any reason?"

"No!"

"Have you ever been committed to a mental institution, gone to a therapist, or taken medication for a mental illness?"

The barrage of questions felt like an attack. "Are you serious?"

"Do you have any problems with drugs, alcohol, gambling, anything like that?"

Whose side was Barbara on? "Absolutely not. Even if I did, I couldn't afford it."

"Do you have any chronic medical problems?"

"No. Would they really use something like that against me?"

"They're ruthless; they'll use anything they can find." Barbara merged onto the main highway going south and pushed the accelerator as far to the floor as it would go. "Do you date? Do men often stay overnight at your house?"

Joy thought about all the things the neighbors had said about her mother even though she hadn't dated for as long as she could remember. Indignation burned her cheeks. Was this the game the Wolffs would play with her? "I had one boyfriend after high school for about two and a half years. We never lived together. He went into the military, and we lost touch. After that, I stayed busy, taking care of my mom. Since she died, I've had a few dates, but not many men in Summer Springs are interested in a bi-racial woman. As you know, the town is ninety-percent white, and fifty percent of them have red necks. The other fifty percent can't get past the fact that my mother wasn't faithful to her husband."

"That brings me to a more sensitive question. How much dirt will these people be able to dig up about your biological father?"

Barbara hit a nerve. The one that stung since the first time Joy was called an ugly name on the playground. They were now passing open fields dotted by an occasional oak tree and reminded her of how she'd often stood alone among the other children in school—never included in their games.

"One of the reasons my mother was ostracized by Jacksonville society is because she refused to name the man. She didn't even tell me when she was on her death bed. If the Wolffs are able to learn his identity, I'd be interested in the information myself."

Barbara passed the sign welcoming them to Summer Springs. "I want you to keep thinking about things like this. I don't want any surprises in the courtroom. If something seems like it might be useful to their case, let me know right away."

Joy's first thought was that she would probably be unable to think of anything else. Her second thought was whether she could really trust Barbara. Outside her role as a lawyer, the woman was known for her love of gossip. Would she be any different?

Gossip was what had ruined her mother—gossip involving Joy's conception. As a result, she'd learned to be very private about her personal life.

"Here we are, home sweet home. Don't forget to

call if you think of anything." Barbara pulled into her parking lot and put the car in park. "In the meantime, I'll see what I can find out about the Wolffs, especially Luca. Damn that man is hot. If I were only twenty years younger, I'd make a play for him. He's certainly able to fill out a pair of trousers. Did you see his butt?" Barbara shook her head. "Maybe that's something you should consider. If you sleep with the tall, dark, and smoking-hot Luca Wolff, it might keep this thing from going to court."

Joy could still hear her laughing after she closed the car door. Barbara might laugh a lot more if she knew how little experience she had in that department. There were made-for-TV movies that made her blush.

She looked around at her modest home. The grass needed mowing. Today's newspaper now lay in a puddle of rain water. One of the local dogs had turned over the garbage can. The mailbox overflowed with sale ads, bogus loan offers, and bills. Would she be able to pay them all this month?

As she unlocked the front door, she noticed the paint chipping. Just as some of the shutters needed repair, and a few shingles had come loose on the roof. The next tropical storm could make things a lot worse.

Joy always considered these things small; they didn't matter. She'd get it taken care of eventually. It was her home, and she was proud to have it. Now, she wondered if it was a good enough home to share with her nephew. He'd spent his first fourteen years in the lap of luxury.

As a little boy, Eric had loved playing in her backyard with second-hand trucks and toy shovels. He was free to dig for worms and get dirty. Her nephew ate peanut butter cookies and colored with markers while she cut Melissa's hair. When it was time to leave, he'd cry and beg to stay.

As Eric got older, he used her old bicycle to meet with the other kids in the neighborhood. He knew them all. Would he still remember them...or her? What would he think of this place now? In the last few years had he become as cynical and judgmental as his father's family?

More important, how had he evolved to committing petty crimes? Surely, he wasn't as bad as Mr. Knight made him sound. Maybe he just needed someone to listen and understand. Could Luca Wolff do that? According to Melissa, Luca had been in charge over a lot of men while he was in the military, but they'd been full-grown marines. They were trained to be tough. Eric was still a boy.

An image came to mind of David and Melissa's wedding reception. Luca hadn't made it to the ceremony. He'd walked into the reception after the dinner plates had been cleared from the tables. In his dress blues, looking so tall, dark, and dangerous, every eye in the place turned to him. Yes, he'd looked dangerous. He'd had a look that said he'd seen too much evil and he'd fought his way through it. His chocolate eyes still held the same look today even though he'd dressed in civilian clothes.

She hadn't had a chance to talk to him fifteen years ago. He'd gone straight to Melissa for a dance. As soon as the music stopped, David joined them. The men were said to be best friends, but the whispered exchange between them seemed heated that day. Oddly, Luca left after only a few minutes and didn't speak to anyone else.

Whatever the source of their disagreement, they must have resolved it. David willed a large sum of money and the guardianship of his only son to Luca.

Why had Melissa chosen her as guardian of Eric? Wouldn't custody be something a married couple discussed and agreed on? She wouldn't know. She'd never gotten close to the altar. But it was a natural assumption.

She walked through the quiet, still house to her bedroom. It had been so long since she'd heard laughter, a welcome, or the words *good night* in these rooms. It wasn't just about what she could do for Eric, but also, how much she needed him.

* * * *

"Did you have a good meeting, sir?"

"It was interesting, to say the least." Luca settled into the back seat of his black SUV and, through the rearview mirror, smiled at Nelson Griffon, his trusted chauffeur and valet. He'd met the starchy Englishman in a Saudi hospital after they'd been injured in separate assaults. After a night of drinking in the courtyard, they'd developed an unbreakable bond. After both men left the military, Luca offered Nelson a job—keeping Luca's affairs in order whenever he was out of the country. Luca wished he had as much faith in his attorney as he did this man. "Have you heard from the rest of the family?" he asked, referring to other, ex-military members of his staff—none of whom were named Wolff.

"Yes, sir. Mrs. Washington is still staying with her sister. Apparently, the woman is driving her mad as her idea of healthy eating is packaged diet meals warmed in the microwave. Her daily activity is low-impact, aqua aerobics and games of mahjong with other widows in her apartment building. Once a week, they go to the senior center for bingo. Mrs. W is eager to return but says, in her own words, *she'd rather drown with a belly full of a cheap chicken by-product than live under your father's roof.* Sorry, sir."

Luca laughed. His housekeeper and cook never failed to speak her mind. It had caused more than a few harsh words between her and Gerald Wolff on one of his rare visits.

"And Arnold, have you heard from him? How is his arm healing?" Arnold, his handyman and groundskeeper, had been injured in the explosion that destroyed their home on Crescent Beach.

Nelson stopped the car at a red light in mid-town. "He's staying with his father and stepmother and says they're taking good care of him, sir. His broken bones are healing nicely, and the cast is ready to be removed from his arm. However, he says the treatment for the burns was torturous. Being in his thirties, it's reasonable that he's concerned about the scarring. He's still hopeful of having a family one day, and he's afraid he won't be presentable to the fairer sex. Personally, I believe the right woman would look past a few scars. His injuries could have been much worse."

A wave of sadness overtook Luca's thoughts. He felt responsible for Arnold's condition. Nelson was right, though. He'd seen many young soldiers permanently disfigured in Afghanistan and Iraq. The least he could do for Arnold was pay his medical bills and provide him with a good income while he recovered. "It's about time we put our household back together, Nelson. Could you help me find a nice five- or six-bedroom house? We may be adding another member to the family."

"An assistant for your writing?"

"My nephew, David, and his wife left behind a fourteen-year-old son."

"Oh my." Nelson offered no further comment on that subject, adding, "I was extremely saddened to hear about the loss of your nephew, sir. I assume he's the gentleman you told me about at our first meeting."

"David was my brother Daniel's only child. We were as thick as thieves, growing up."

"I'll do my best to find a suitable home to include the boy, sir."

"Thank you, Nelson. And remember, I don't want a condominium. I must have total privacy."

"Not to worry, sir," Nelson assured him as they pulled into his father's circular drive.

Luca hated the thought of walking through the double oak doors. When he'd left for the Marine Corps, he swore he'd never sleep under its roof again.

"Home sweet home."

Chapter Five

Tuesday, August 14—The Judge

Joy waited impatiently for news regarding Eric. She'd been repeatedly refused a visit or even a phone call with him. All Barbara's attempts to make the Juvenile Detention Center see reason had also failed. Finally, on Friday afternoon, following her meeting with Michael Knight, she received a letter from the Duval County Family Court. It stated that she would appear in Judge Alexander Benedict's office this Tuesday at three-thirty.

She'd been waiting for a total of eight days, but only had three days to inform Barbara and prepare. Those last few days had flown by. All of her Tuesday afternoon appointments had to be rescheduled, some on Sunday, her only day off. She'd had to buy something to wear with the tips she'd earned on that extra day. Barbara had called three times to ask her the same uncomfortable, intrusive questions she'd asked on the drive home from Knight's office. Mostly, Barbara wanted to talk, like a teenager at a slumber party, about Luca Wolff. At least Joy hadn't had enough time to let her nerves fray...until now.

Joy's confidence took a hard hit when Barbara picked her up, wearing a smart gray pantsuit, then admonishing Joy for her choice in the dress she wore for meeting a judge who would decide custody of Eric. It was an old garment, found at a flea market, but she loved the full skirt and vivid colors. Furthermore, her lawyer didn't realize how short she was on time and resources.

Barbara rolled her eyes. "You look like you're ready for a calypso party."

Joy didn't know what she'd meant by that and assumed it wasn't a compliment. However, Barbara's wild driving soon distracted her. The trip seemed much shorter than the first time, now that she dreaded facing Luca Wolff and his attorney again. They scared her more than meeting the judge.

When the two men walked in, wearing designer suits, her already low confidence took a deeper nosedive. Michael Knight looked downright smarmy. She'd have more trust in a boxful of snakes. But Luca was heart-skippingly handsome when he nodded at her. Why were men like him allowed to look so good? Wasn't it enough that they had more money than the national treasury?

Four chairs lined up in precision order in front of a massive mahogany desk. She took the chair farthest to the left. It was close to the door. She felt safer there. Barbara sat beside her squeezing a large shoulder bag between them. Michael Knight took the other center seat, leaving the chair at the far right for Luca Wolff.

Knight leaned toward Barbara. "Have you ever been before Judge Benedict?"

"I can't say I have."

He settled back and crossed his arms, an all-knowing expression covering his smug face. "Let me warn you, you can expect anything. He's the most unconventional judge on the bench. You might even say he's eccentric."

"That may work in our favor."

Knight smirked. "I said he was unconventional and eccentric, Ms. Allgood, not stupid."

Luca gave the lawyer a weary glance. "Knight, stop harassing that woman."

Suddenly, the door flew open, and a tall, stocky, African-American man strode in. He removed his black robe and placed it on a hanger in the closet. Beneath it, he wore a salmon-colored polo shirt, khaki shorts, and sneakers. "Sorry, I'm late. My court session ran long."

He then pulled out a set of golf clubs from the bottom of the same closet and sat them beside his chair. "These are to remind you that I have plans this afternoon."

Michael Knight rose and smoothed his tie. "We won't take too much of your time, Your Honor."

The judge lifted a brow. "You won't take *any* of my time, Mr. Knight. This isn't a courtroom; please sit down. I'm only interested in speaking to the principles of this case. Unless I ask you a question, you can check your emails."

"But Your Honor, my client—" Barbara began.

The judge leaned forward to eye Barbara, suspicion in his eyes. "Who are you?"

"My name is Barbara Allgood, Your Honor. I represent Miss Sullivan."

"What didn't you understand about what I just said to Mr. Knight? Please have a seat."

In Joy's mind, Barbara's body seemed to deflate as she sank into her chair.

The judge opened a folder and leafed through the papers inside. "I studied this file in bed last night. A screwed-up mess is what this is. How do two people living in the same home let something like this happen? We're not talking about who gets the antique china. Eric is a flesh-and-blood child." He looked up at Joy and Luca in turn. "By the way, you have my deepest condolences for your loss."

"Thank you, Your Honor." Luca took the lead. "I believe this started when my nephew and his wife decided to end their marriage. They hadn't gotten along for some time, as I understand. The trip they were on when the accident happened was planned to initiate their divorce."

"You'll notice, Your Honor," Knight interrupted. "Mr. David Wolff's will was signed when the boy was only a week old. Apparently, the couple agreed on some things at that time."

Barbara jumped in. "Mrs. Wolff's will bears a more recent date, Your Honor. As the mother, she knew more about what her son's needs were."

The judge narrowed his eyes on the two attorneys. "If you two kids don't let the grown-ups handle this, you'll be sent to wait in the hall. Do you understand?"

Both attorneys nodded silently.

Judge Benedict looked back and forth between Luca and Joy. "What does the boy have to say?"

Joy rushed to be first to answer. "Sir, I called the detention center and was told I wasn't on his list of visitors. They wouldn't even let me speak to him on the phone. My attorney has even left messages with my congressman and the governor's office."

The judge's brow knit in concern. "When did you

see Eric last?"

"I haven't been allowed to see him since my mother, his grandmother, died three years ago. He had just turned twelve at the time."

"You don't seem very old yourself, Miss Sullivan," the judge observed.

"I'll be thirty years old next month, old enough to have a family of my own."

"Interesting," the judge quipped. "Why do you think you'd be the better guardian for your nephew?"

As the judge stared at her, Joy could see he cared about her answer—he also cared about Eric. Instinct told her he was a fair man. She didn't hesitate to answer. "I have a stable home, good values, and I can give him the love and attention he may have been missing before. That's the only reason I can think of for Eric to have gotten into so much trouble."

Luca crossed his arms and huffed.

The judge looked his way. "You disagree, Mr. Wolff? What is your take on the boy?"

"He was brought up spoiled and coddled. He doesn't need more of the same. What he needs is a strong role model."

"Don't you mean rules and discipline like a marine, Mr. Wolff?" Joy could barely believe she'd said it out loud, but now she was angered. "He isn't one of your soldiers. He needs to learn how to behave in society, not on the battlefield."

"Sometimes it feels the same," Luca remarked. "He needs to learn to be an honorable man. Until he is, I can keep him in the lifestyle which he's more accustomed. He's already lost his parents. There's no need for him to lose everything else."

Joy was so mad, she had to squeeze both hands together to keep them from shaking. There was no way to hide the tears in her eyes.

"How is he taking the loss of his parents?" the judge asked Luca.

The muscles in Luca's jaws tightened. "I'm also not on his list of approved visitors, but my brother, Eric's grandfather, said he'd speak to the boy after we received the news two weeks ago. I haven't heard how it went. Daniel's been in Tampa since that time, planning for David and Melissa's...return. I haven't been able to contact him. I don't have a clue what is taking so long.

Judge Benedict's brows curled over his narrowed eyes. "Do I understand this correctly? You're not Eric's uncle, but his great-uncle?"

Luca took a deep breath and frowned. "Yes. I was a product of my father's second marriage, so David, though he was my age, was actually my nephew."

The judge tapped his fingers on the desk as he looked back and forth between Luca and her. "I guess there's no way the two of you are going to agree on which of you will gain custody of this boy. And since neither of you has been in contact with him, I'll have to talk to him myself. Let them try to give me some bull about not being on a list.

"The next time I see you will be in the courtroom." He looked at his calendar. "That will be on this coming Monday at one o'clock. In the meantime, I want his custody decided before his release next week."

Joy watched the judge wheel his golf bag from the room and realized that the next time they were all together, the mud would fly. As her parentage was the

35

only thing anyone could dig up about her, it would be exposed to all. Would it be enough to turn the judge against her? He seemed like a fair man, but he could have traditional ideas.

Barbara rose and tugged her oversized purse onto her shoulder. "Sorry, kid, but I won't be able to take you home. I still have a few things to do here in town. If you hurry, you can make the next bus to Summer Springs." She removed her wallet, looked Joy up and down, and then handed her a five-dollar bill. "This should be enough for the fare. Try to find something decent to wear next week."

Joy rushed from the room humiliated. She caught the sound of a man laughing behind her. It never got easier, being made fun of.

****

Luca sat in a silent rage all the way back to his father's house on the other side of Jacksonville. He didn't care to look out at the throng of cars and perspiring pedestrians lining the city streets. The afternoon heat was ridiculous. He'd removed his jacket as soon as he'd left the courthouse. Thank God for back-row air-conditioning vents. Why hadn't he offered Joy Sullivan a ride home? The bus must be miserable.

It was lucky that he wasn't driving himself. The temptation to run over a lawyer or two would have been too strong to resist. There'd been no need for that Allgood woman to embarrass Joy Sullivan in that manner. When Knight laughed, he'd nearly punched him in the face. It was a relief to know this would be over in another week. By then, he hoped to be moving into his new home—and in the market for his own attorney.

He did feel sorry for Miss Sullivan's situation, but still didn't think she had the resources needed to raise his nephew. Besides money, it would require strength and an understanding of the teenage male mind. It had been nearly twenty years, but he remembered those days well. Besides that, he'd led soldiers into battle who weren't much older than Eric. He knew how fragile their egos were and how to build their confidence. Male bonding was a serious issue. Thinking back, he realized that those all-important life lessons had been provided by paid staff.

Perhaps Eric had missed out on having a strong role model. Maybe David had, as well. His brother, Daniel, hadn't been any better at parenting than his own father, something Luca didn't come to realize until he was older. They say abuse could be handed down in a family. As far as he was concerned, neglect could be as severe as beatings.

As far as Joy Sullivan was concerned, he didn't begrudge her the money Melissa had left her. She could certainly use it. But she'd have to be happy with regular visits from Eric. He had no problem with offering her that, as long as Eric agreed.

"Nelson, as soon as I have keys to the new house, I want you to send for Mrs. Washington. She needs to collect all of Eric's belongings. I don't want him to have to go back to his empty house right away."

Nelson cleared his throat as he glanced at Luca in the rearview mirror. "I took the liberty of looking into it yesterday. I'm afraid that won't be possible, sir. The house has already been closed and cleaned out."

"Who ordered that?"

Nelson pulled the car to a stop at a red light before

answering. "Your father, sir. His maids told me he had everything thrown out. They confided in me that a few pictures and keepsakes were saved by Mr. David's staff before they were dismissed. They thought Master Eric might want them someday. I have their contact information."

A car horn blared behind them the minute the light turned green. Nelson lowered his window to wave his middle finger at the driver before moving forward. Luca laughed. His friend was becoming more American every day.

Nelson continued as though nothing had happened. "I'm sure the young man won't mind updating his wardrobe."

"Damn, I don't even know what size clothes the kid wears." The mention of clothes gave Luca another thought. "I'd like you to run an errand for me tomorrow, Nelson."

Chapter Six

Wednesday, August 15—Eric

Eric didn't mind that his lunch had been interrupted. This place made the worst spaghetti he'd ever eaten. It was just pasta and hamburger meat in a puddle of red grease. The garlic bread was stale on the outside, chewy on the inside. The meal was accompanied by a small piece of yellow cake left over from World War Two. Even the glass of lukewarm orange drink didn't help him swallow the dried cake. He'd give anything for a pizza and cold soda from Luigi's. That was the first place he intended to head for when he got out of here next week.

It had been two weeks since he last had a visitor. After he was arrested, his dad went on a rant about tough love and making him fend for himself, so he never showed. That was okay. Eric was sick of hearing his father's lectures about making him into a man. As far as Eric was concerned, his father wasn't setting a good example. His dad worked all day as a yes-man for his own dad and grandfather. Not to say he was soft. From what Eric heard, his father was ruthless when it came to cheating small-business people out of their life's work. There had even been times when his friend's families had folded and disappeared because of his dad's big business deals. Eric had no intention of following in those footsteps.

Then there was the women. Hookers, his mother called them, there for the money. It was humiliating when a picture of his father showed up in the newspaper with one of those women wrapped around him. They wore too-tight clothes, too much makeup, and fake boobs. The articles would talk about the *Wolff charm* and make a veiled mention of the wife waiting at home. His father rarely came home anymore. He cared more about who to screw next—either in the boardroom or bedroom.

Eric's mom had slipped in for a visit a few times and put money in his canteen account. That is, when she was sober and remembered he was there. She never stayed too long and usually left after her hands started to shake. She was drunk so much of the time, her skin had the permanent smell of alcohol. It seeped into her sweat and out her pores even if she hadn't had a drink that morning. While he was locked up, he worried about her. Was anyone checking on her, making sure she didn't pass out with a lit cigarette in her hand? Since he wasn't there, who would clean her up after she puked? He hated doing those things for her. It wasn't a job for a kid. But he felt sorry for her.

Yes, his so-called privileged life was a friggin' fairy tale.

No one here knew anything about him or his home life. No one cared. He wore the same orange, draw-string pants, rubber slippers, and white JDC T-shirts as the rest. White socks and underwear looked about the same no matter where you bought them or how much you paid. His small size made him a prime target as it was. If they found out his family had money, he'd get pushed around and harassed by the bigger guys even worse. They'd want stuff he could buy from the canteen. They might even want information about his family's homes and security systems.

When the guard led him around a corner to the visiting room, Eric saw a man waiting. He was a humongous, older black guy Eric had never seen before. The scowl on the man's face contradicted the wildly colored Hawaiian print shirt he wore. The hair suddenly stood up on the back of his neck. Whatever this was about wasn't good. Had they changed their minds about releasing him next week? Had his dad decided to send him to that boarding school he'd been threatening? He slowed his steps to a standstill, but the guard grabbed his arm to make him keep moving.

The big guy stood and motioned to a chair across from him. "Have a seat, Eric. I'm Judge Alexander Benedict. Do you know why I'm here?"

"A judge? I already had my hearing about borrowing that car from the neighbor's house. I was just supposed to serve ninety days and pay restitution. I don't know what I'm supposed to pay back. I didn't damage the car. If they want money for the gas I used, they can have whatever is in my account here. I don't have anything else." He was babbling like a girl. How embarrassing was that?

"Thanks for the offer." Benedict sat down and leaned against the back of the chair. "I'll find out if you owe anything. But that's not what I've come to talk about. I'm here regarding your parents' last wishes."

Eric panicked. He lifted his hands palms out even though he wore handcuffs. "No, no, no! My mom said she wouldn't let Dad send me away. Don't tell me he got to her. Damn! She must have been too drunk to understand. I don't want to go."

The judge's eyes widened as he sat straighter. "Calm down, kid. I don't have a clue what you're talking about. Didn't your grandfather tell you why I'm here?"

Eric's shoulders relaxed, but he still felt apprehensive. "Like my grandfather would walk across the street to talk to me. I haven't seen that old coot since last Christmas. He hates kids. My dad was probably a nasty accident."

The judge looked a little sick. "You don't know. Your Uncle Luca and Aunt Joy have both tried to speak to you. They weren't on the approved visitors list. I sure as hell wish they had been."

"Look, I don't know what you're talking about. Are you sure you have the right person? I'm Eric Wolff. My parents are David and Melissa Wolff. They're in Mexico, as far as I know. I haven't seen my aunt or uncle in years. Why would they want to see me now?"

The judge leaned closer and folded his hands, "I'm just going to have to give it to you straight, kid. Your parents are gone. I have to decide where you're going to go from here."

"No problem," Eric assured him. "They never stay away for long. I'll just stay with our housekeeper. I stay with her all the time. I promise I won't do anything stupid. I won't even leave the property."

"No. I guess I didn't say it right. Your parents..."

"Wait a minute. I know what this is about." Eric felt a wave of anger. "They promised there wouldn't be a custody battle. They promised. This divorce was supposed to be easy. They said they had agreed to share custody."

"No, kid, they're really gone. They aren't coming back. There was an accident. Don't you watch the news?"

Eric's mind felt like a gumball machine after a coin was inserted. His thoughts were jumbling together and falling out. "I watch basketball. Nobody here watches the news."

The judge jumped out of his chair and yelled for the guard. "Get this boy his clothes and have him ready to leave with me in thirty minutes. I want to see the warden...now!"

Chapter Seven

Wednesday, August 15—The Courtroom

Joy had just returned to her house with her two shopping bags. Her last two appointments had canceled, and for the first time, she wasn't worried about the lost income. A young man from a messenger service came to her door that morning and handed her a large padded envelope. Inside was five hundred dollars in cash and an unsigned note.

I'm sorry for your loss. I hope this money helps with your expenses for the funeral.

Yes, it was charity, but how could she return the money when she didn't know who sent it? It was probably one of her customers who'd known Melissa. If she did find out who this benefactor was, she'd return the money when her inheritance came…if it was ever paid. A substantial windfall seemed unlikely for someone with her bad luck. Look what her life had been like so far.

She'd bought herself an appropriate outfit at a nearby consignment shop and put a bouquet of flowers on hold at the florist for Melissa's funeral. She left about four hundred in her bank account. She'd toyed with the idea of getting a buy-as-you-go cell phone, but that would be another monthly bill, and the shop needed a new window air conditioner, which was more important.

The phone by her bed rang. She reached for the pen and notepad beside it. "Southern Style Salon, Joy speaking. How can I help you?"

"Where have you been?" Barbara sounded stressed. "The judge's bailiff called. Benedict wants us in his courtroom no later than six o'clock. He says it's urgent—and it must be because hearings are usually over by five-thirty. Put on your Sunday-go-to-meeting clothes, honey, and I'll be over in twenty minutes."

Thirty minutes later, she'd barely gotten both feet inside Barbara's small economy car when it reversed out of her driveway, kicking up gravel. She quickly closed the door and tugged on her seat belt. "What is this about? Did the bailiff say?"

"No, but he said the judge meant business. It sounds like he has a bee under his robes. Are you sure you're not hiding anything from me?"

"As I told you before, there's nothing to hide."

It was precisely five thirty-five when they rushed through the doors of the courthouse where two security guards waited. The man waved Barbara to his side while the female put Joy's handbag into a basket that carried it through an x-ray machine. She ran a wand around her body while Joy held her arms out, then discreetly removed a price tag from her zipper pull. Joy smiled gratefully before running to catch up to Barbara at the elevators.

They walked through the door of courtroom number four in time to see Judge Benedict facing off with another man in black robes.

"Dammit, Alex, you can't just commandeer a

courtroom the minute it's empty. You have to schedule these things. Why do you have to be so impulsive?"

"This is a matter of life or death," Benedict told him.

"If the case is that serious, where is your jury?"

"Right here," the judge said as he held up a huge balled fist. "I just may decide to kill somebody before I leave today."

"I'm out of here," the other man conceded.

Joy and her lawyer quietly took seats at one of the front tables. They watched the judge pace back and forth in front of his bench until Luca Wolff and Michael Knight arrived five minutes later. Both looked like they could model for GQ, of course. Did they wear anything besides Italian suits?

"You lied to me," Benedict bellowed, pointing a thick finger at Luca.

Joy was relieved not to be the target of his anger.

Outraged, Luca bellowed right back. "I do not tell lies, sir."

"You said your brother would notify Eric that his parents had died. Two weeks have passed since the accident, two weeks!"

"Sir, my father, the chief of police for Jacksonville, and one of his detectives were all in the room when Daniel said he'd take care of it. They can tell you." Luca ran both hands down his face and then hit the table top with them. "Damn! My brother is such a dick!"

"That may be, but it doesn't help how I felt this afternoon when I had to give him the news." The judge walked around his bench and slumped into his chair.

"This kind of shit just ain't my job."

Joy leaped out of her chair. "Is Eric okay? I need to see him. Is there any way I can get on that ridiculous list?"

"Oh, you're going to see him all right," Judge Benedict sneered. "He's in the back room. After delivering such devastating news, I couldn't just leave him in that place. Take a seat, all of you. We have to figure out where young Eric is going from here. I can't exactly take him home with me. I already have five kids, three of whom are still teenagers. My wife would have me drawn and quartered."

In a quandary, Luca had to think fast. He couldn't take Eric to his father's house. The old man and Daniel would eat the boy alive. But he'd just received the keys to his new home a few hours ago. It would take at least a week to get utilities set up and have it furnished. How had he gotten into this mess? Was this an indication of how parenthood was going to be?

The courtroom fell silent for a few minutes. Even though the judge wore a Hawaiian shirt instead of black robes, he presented an authoritative persona. "Mr. Wolff, our report indicated that you've recently separated from the military and you write novels for a living. You've traveled extensively in the last few years. What kind of impact do you suppose that lifestyle will have on Eric's routine?"

Michael Knight rose and fastened a button on his jacket preparing to answer. Before he could get a word out, the judge leaned forward and raised his hand to stop him. "Have a seat, Knight. This isn't a trial. I want to hear from your client directly. Everyone stays seated."

"Your Honor," Luca began, "I've spoken to my agent and my publisher about limiting my promotional tours to the summer months. I think it'll be good for Eric to experience new places while he's on vacation from school. I work mainly at home from a personal computer. As far as time spent in meetings and local events, I have a small personal staff to take care of him. He won't be left alone for a moment. All I need is a little time to get everything ready. Eric and I could stay in a hotel until then."

Benedict shook his head. "I don't know. This kid's world is upside down right now. A hotel seems awfully impersonal." He turned to Joy. "What about you, Miss Sullivan. You work from home, too. Wouldn't Eric interfere with your business?"

"I've converted my garage into a hair salon. A door in my kitchen leads to the shop, but my clients come in through a separate entrance. Eric would be perfectly safe to do homework, watch television, or even have a friend in. He can get to me at any time, and I can check on him throughout the day. By the way, Summer Springs High School has recently been renovated, and I think Eric will be pleased there."

Luca shook his head. "That's not acceptable, Your Honor. Every Wolff man since the civil war has attended West Glen Academy." He turned to face Joy. "Of course, that wouldn't mean anything to you, Miss Sullivan. But you can't have him going to a public school in the suburbs."

"Hey! I went to public school." Joy pursed her lips and glared at him.

"I rest my case." Luca smirked. It was crunch-time, and the gloves were coming off. He hadn't appreciated the judge's implication that he couldn't provide Eric with a pleasant environment. He had no intention of losing his right to give his nephew a proper education.

The judge struck his gavel three times. "Mr. Wolff, I'll have you know that I attended public school from kindergarten through high school and after that spent two years in a community college. I'm not impressed by your arrogance. Furthermore, due to past behaviors, West Glen has decided to release Eric from their program."

Luca was shocked at the anger he felt for his alma mater. "I can speak to them, sir. Perhaps he'll turn his behavior around once he's in a different home environment. I'm sure they'll be willing to give him a second chance."

"He's had several chances already, Mr. Wolff. And I don't like the way this hearing is going." Benedict sat back. "Each of your attorneys has two minutes to convince me why their client is the best guardian for Eric. I repeat, two minutes. You'd better make it good."

Luca's attorney rose to make his case.

"Your Honor, David Wolff named my client, his uncle, as Eric's guardian in a will he had drawn up only a week after the boy was born. There's no indication that he'd wavered from that decision in almost fifteen years. We feel his wishes should take precedence. Luca Wolff is willing and capable. He has the resources and maturity needed to care for a troubled teenage boy."

"Get real, Mr. Knight," the judge scoffed. "Neither of these two people have a clue about what they're getting into."

Barbara Allgood took her turn to be heard. "Your Honor, Joy Sullivan has a strong maternal instinct and sense of family values. Eric is her last remaining relative. In addition, Melissa Wolff felt my client would make a responsible guardian for her son as she stated in her will, which I should point out, was drawn up more recently. I should also point out, Mrs. Wolff knew what the challenges would be when she made her decision."

The judge banged his gavel again and bellowed louder. "I've heard all this before. I'm going to take a break and talk to Eric. I'll give this more thought and have a decision for you when I return." Judge Benedict stood and left the courtroom.

"Here's where things are going to get interesting," Knight whispered. "There's no telling what he'll do next."

Chapter Eight

Wednesday, August 15—Court Orders

When the judge walked back into his office, Eric looked up from the borrowed computer tablet he'd been using to play a game. "Hey, dude. What's going on out there?"

"You can't be calling me dude, dude." Benedict winked then sank onto the sofa next to Eric. "It's bad for my kick-ass rep. You gotta call me Judge, Your Honor, or sir."

"Okay, Judge-Your-Honor-sir, are my Aunt Joy and Uncle Luca out there?"

"Yeah, and it's starting to get a little tense. Both want you a lot. I don't know which way to go. Those two people are opposites. I don't suppose you have any thoughts about the problem?"

Eric laid the tablet on the table and turned on the sofa to face the judge. "Not really. I've been thinking about it some, though. Neither of them had much to do with me up until now. I wouldn't be surprised if they were fighting about which of them would get stuck with me. It must have something to do with my money."

"You're fourteen. How much money could you have?"

"I'm loaded. I don't have cash, but I've got like

three trust funds from different family members. You have to remember; I'm the only one in the family of my generation. I've had people leave me money who I never even met. But it's either leave the money to me or a cat shelter. By the way, that has happened, too. My parents are gone. I can't access the money myself, but my guardian can. They'd get like a maintenance allowance from some guy at the bank who takes care of that stuff."

The judge folded his arms and tilted his head. "How do you know this?"

"My family doesn't talk about anything but money. It's an obsession—like a soldier who only talks about war or a farmer who only talks about corn." Eric returned his attention to the computer game.

"If you had to pick between your aunt and your uncle, which would you choose and why?" Benedict asked.

Eric shrugged. "I don't know. What does it matter? I'm going to do my own thing either way."

The judge raised one brow. "Is that what you've been doing...your own thing?"

The game in Eric's hand made a maniacal laughing sound. "Yeah, and it works for me."

"You're going to be fifteen in a few weeks, right Eric?"

Eric shrugged again. "Yeah."

"So, the next time you're arrested you'll be put in level three?"

"I suppose." Eric didn't want to play anymore. He began picking at the rubber edge around the sole of his shoe.

Judge Benedict continued. "So those kids are

between fifteen and eighteen. I hear that a lot of them are pretty big guys—like bodybuilders. The crimes they've committed are sometimes more serious, armed robbery, rape, murder. Some of them are waiting to go to real prison. Aren't you afraid of the way they may treat you? Let's face it. You're a little small for your age."

Eric frowned. "I'm tougher than I look."

"I sure hope so."

"I guess if I had to choose—hell, I don't know. I don't suppose you offer a test drive."

The judge stared at him for a minute, then stood. "That might be a good idea. Do you want to go back in there with me?"

****

Eric sat in the witness chair at the side of the judge's bench. He looked out at the only two people in the room he knew. He hadn't seen them in a very long time and didn't know either of them well, but he'd be leaving with one of them. His stomach tightened.

The judge gestured to the table at the right. "Mr. Wolff, you may say a few words to Eric before we begin if you like."

"Yes, Your Honor."

Luca looked at Eric with a serious expression. "I haven't had a chance to tell you how sorry I am about your parents. I'm also sorry that I haven't stayed in touch. We have a lot of time to make up for that now. I promise everything is going to be all right, no matter what happens today."

Eric just stared at him. How many promises had been made to him and then broken? He admired his uncle. From what he'd heard, Luca was a badass who'd bucked the family traditions and made a name for himself on the battlefield and through his writing about those experiences. Luca was tough, but maybe too tough. He didn't know. They'd never even had a conversation.

Judge Benedict then nodded to Joy. "Is there anything you'd like to say, Miss Sullivan?"

His Aunt Joy nearly leaped forward, looking like she wanted to reach out to him. "Eric, I love you. I don't care how much time has passed or how old you are. I'll always love you."

He felt a lump form in his throat. Why did women have to be so mushy? Joy had treated him good when he was a kid. She gave him fresh-baked cookies that were better than the ones at home. But he wasn't a baby anymore. Did Joy understand that? A lot of time had passed.

"Okay then," Judge Benedict began. "Now that the reunion is over, we can move on to the reason we're here. I've never been involved in such a stupid mess. We have a half-grown boy with two possible guardians. He doesn't have a relationship with either one of you. I don't know how that happened, and at this point, it doesn't matter." The judge sat up and leaned forward. "This is what I do know. Eric has made some bad choices. Boys his age tend to do that especially when they aren't getting the attention and guidance they need. I do not doubt that Miss Sullivan can devote endless maternal attention to him."

Luca huffed. "When she isn't closed up in her shop."

Joy glared at him. "I told you, there is a door he'd have access through at any time."

Judge Benedict's voice rose. "However, Miss Sullivan, Mr. Wolff could provide the masculine guidance that he needs."

Joy crossed her arms and turned to the side. "Or his servants can."

Luca clenched his teeth. "My staff are well-paid, much-respected employees, not servants."

Eric pounded a fist on the railing. "Order in the court."

"That's my job." The judge turned back to the adults. "While you ponder that, let me tell you what my take is on the boy. He's intelligent, quick-witted, and resourceful. He's also insecure and has no sense of self-worth."

"I object," Eric whined.

The judge rolled his eyes. "He has all the material things a boy his age could ever want, but as these conflicting wills prove, he's been emotionally neglected. I'm sorry to say this, Miss Sullivan. I know you loved your sister. But I believe his parents were more concerned with the differences between them than they were with their son—their only child."

Eric lifted both hands above his head. "Amen."

"Quiet, you." The judge sat back again and studied his folded fingers. "What Eric needs most is a combination of what the two of you have to offer."

Luca quickly responded. "We can do that. We can share custody of Eric. Kids from divorced parents do it every day."

Joy's head bobbed up and down in agreement. All she needed to plead her case were her large dewy eyes Eric thought.

The judge shook his head. "You're talking about

kids who are secure in the knowledge they're loved and wanted. Even then, it doesn't always work. How do I know that the two of you can get along and cooperate? I haven't seen any evidence of it so far."

Joy pleaded, "You have to let us try. What other option does Eric have?"

Judge Benedict flattened his hands together as though he were praying for an answer. "I've got a lot to say and no one here is going to be delighted to hear any of it, but it's not up for debate. I've come to a decision. Everyone will stay in their seats and hear me out, no matter how long-winded I get. Questions are welcome when I've finished, but arguments are not. Does everyone understand?" There was no reply. "Okay, girls and boys, this is the way it's going to go."

Benedict rubbed his hands together and smiled. "Eric is going to take you both on a little test drive…sixty days to be exact. This period will give him time to get to know you and find out which parenting plan works best for him. Now, don't think that he'll be making this decision on his own. He'll be keeping a nightly journal of his activities, his feelings, and his progress."

When Eric groaned, the judge pointed at him. "I told you to be quiet." Benedict continued. "Every Friday after school, he'll turn those pages over to Dr. Bennett Johnson, his therapist. He has a standing appointment, courtesy of the state."

"No way!" Eric exclaimed.

"Kid, how good do you think you look in a white T-shirt and orange pants with a drawstring holding them up?"

Eric decided to keep his mouth shut before he got

in deeper and maybe wouldn't get out.

"Dr. Johnson will then hand those pages over to me with his weekly report. You'll also have random visits from his social worker, Larry Meyers. Mr. Meyers will be made aware of the special circumstances. He works with troubled kids every day and will probably have some pointers. Take advantage of that. You didn't have the luxury of fourteen years to prepare for this."

Luca raised an index finger and cleared his throat.

"A question already," the judge quipped. "What's on your mind, Mr. Wolff?"

"Sir, you mentioned school. Eric will need to get back into the classroom as soon as possible. How do you suggest Miss Sullivan and I divide our time with him?"

"That's an excellent question...and brings us to the good part." Benedict paused with a sly grin. "For all of you to get to know each other and come up with a workable game plan, you'll be living together for the next couple of months."

Luke offered a suggestion. "I have plenty of room, Your Honor, but my house won't be ready to live in for at least a week."

"Wait a minute!" Joy interrupted. "I have to work, too. I can't afford to take a bus back and forth from Jacksonville every day."

Judge Benedict tapped his gavel. "You make a good point, Miss Sullivan. Your salon isn't exactly mobile, but Mr. Wolff's computer and cell phone are." He turned to face Luca with an expression of satisfaction. "You'll all be living in Miss Sullivan's house in Summer Springs. You have twenty-four hours to get started. Since you don't have proper accommodations for Eric, Mr. Wolff, he can spend tonight with Miss Sullivan."

Luca's face reddened.

Judge Benedict smiled and spread his hands out to each side. "Consider it a co-parent project."

Eric broke out in delighted laughter. "This is going to be a blast!"

Chapter Nine

Thursday, August 16—The Beginning

Joy didn't sleep well. She and Eric had shared a pizza and went to bed early. She needn't have bothered. Joy had tossed all night, fighting the urge to check on him, certain it was a case of shell shock. Her orderly little life had just been thrown into chaos.

She couldn't believe he was right across the hall in her old bedroom. She'd cleaned it out, all but the twin bed and dresser, when she took over her mother's room. She didn't blame him for looking a little stunned when he first saw the empty room, but she'd told him he could do whatever he liked to decorate it. That put a smile on his face.

Eric wasn't the sweet chubby-cheeked boy she remembered. His features were more angular, almost gaunt. He was too thin, but if his appetite for pizza was any indication, that could change. He'd slipped up and used a curse word a couple of times but apologized immediately. Maybe he'd be able to drop that habit on his own. Speaking of habits, he'd wandered into the backyard twice and came back smelling like cigarette smoke. She'd decided not to bring it up on his first night. However, smoking was something she couldn't allow.

What bothered her most were his eyes. Those warm chocolate eyes looked haunted even when his conversation was animated. She wasn't the only one whose world had turned upside down. He'd lost both his home and his parents. It was her job to ease him through this transition. Or, she should say, her and Luca Wolff's job.

That was another subject that kept her awake. What was she going to do with that man in her house for two months? What would he think of her humble little bungalow? All she could think to do was welcome him and be the hostess her mother had taught her to be. She planned to prepare her mother's room for him, temporarily, and she'd sleep on the sofa. If he wasn't comfortable, he could leave.

What seemed like minutes after she'd finally fallen to sleep, her phone began ringing.

"I think we can put a cautious check mark in the win column." Barbara Allgood stated smugly. "You're the one that won home-field advantage. You'll have your support system all around you. And you'll blow Mr. Perfect right out of the water."

Joy didn't want to point out that she didn't have a support system. She didn't even have friends. She had clients. Summer Springs had grown up enough over the years to be more tolerant of racial differences, but her mother's shame was never forgotten. Her mother had been beautiful, elegant, sophisticated, and married to a white man. Even though they'd lived in Jacksonville when Joy was born, word of her mother's affair with a man of color had followed them to Summer Springs. Many of the people in town worked or had family in the city. They at least read the gossip in the local society pages about the Sullivan divorce after her birth. The respectable citizens of Summer Springs looked at Joy with the same jaundiced eye that Luca Wolff and his family did. And now, he was going to be her house guest.

"I have no intention of making an enemy of Mr. Wolff. The judge expects us to learn to get along and work together—for Eric's sake."

Barbara chuckled. "Yeah, that's going to happen. Believe me, honey; he won't last a week in the burbs. What you have to do is gain little Eric's affections so that he doesn't fly the coop with his uncle. Keeping him in your house would be a definite advantage."

Joy didn't like Barbara's snide tone. "What do you mean?"

"Well, it's obvious. The Wolffs may turn their backs on the little brat, but he's still one of them. They're not going to let him do without all the luxuries they can afford. It would be bad for their reputations. Do you think they'll want to find their fine family on the front page of the tabloids?"

People like Barbara amazed Joy. She seemed to loathe the upper-class yet dreamed of nothing but being one of them.

"That grungy outfit Eric was wearing yesterday proves my point," Barbara continued. "They must have spent as much for those rags as you make in a month. If you're really lucky, they may be willing to shell out enough to pay for a boarding school overseas somewhere. That would put a lid on any gossip he might cause them. I'm surprised he hasn't been shipped off already."

Joy suddenly hated Barbara Allgood, but she was a

client of the salon. Joy couldn't afford to lose even one client. Barbara had offered her legal services for free, just to be able to tie herself to a case involving the Wolff family. Joy had been aware of that, but she didn't know any other lawyers, and she didn't have a lot of money. She'd been desperate. She decided that it would be best to keep her mouth shut, but she'd prove Barbara wrong. She planned to do all she could to make Eric happy to stay without the benefit of Wolff money.

"It sounds like Eric is awake. I should let you go so I can make him some breakfast."

"That's right," Barbara laughed. "Keep the little monster happy. I'll see you at my regular time."

How dare she call Eric a monster and a brat? He was just a little boy—well, a teenaged boy…with oversized, street gangster clothes, long, stringy, died black hair, and a slightly abrasive attitude. But those huge dark eyes underneath melted her heart.

How would Barbara like it if all her hair fell out? She could make it happen. But it wasn't even worth thinking. If that happened, she'd lose all her other clients and Barbara would sue her.

****

Luca was delighted to learn that the rest of his staff had hopped on the first flights back after Nelson called them. They arrived last night ready to work.

It humbled him to know they preferred to be together in his house than anywhere separately. They truly were a family. It would be interesting to see how this two-month glitch would affect everyone. Miss Sullivan had the impression they were servants. She'd find out differently.

He left Nelson in charge of getting the others up to

speed with this temporary arrangement while he went to the mall. All he needed were a few clothes for Eric until they could go shopping together.

He watched throngs of teenagers mill the center area of the mall, eating, laughing, and eating more. Finally, a small group wandered into a store displaying shoes and clothing. He followed and wondered how anyone could make good choices under colored strobe lights and pulsing music. A girl with half her hair shaved and wearing black lipstick approached him.

"Can I help you, sir?"

Luca had never felt as old as he did in that minute. "I have no idea. My nephew needs a couple of outfits. He's fourteen and about your size. He likes baggy things. I don't think he'll be going anywhere special, just hanging around the house."

"No problem. Sizes are flexible in most of our styles. Does your nephew need shoes?"

He left with a pair of jeans and two shirts twice the size Luca would wear. The girl also insisted he'd need a package of boxers and a hat with a strange looking skull on the front.

When he drove his personal car onto Joy's parking lot, he saw his large black SUV parked by her side door. He figured it had something to do with her anxious expression as she rushed toward him. "Your people are here, and they're poking around all over my house. It feels like the secret service has arrived in advance of a presidential visit."

Luca would have laughed if he hadn't been so distracted by the exterior view of her tiny house. She had some kind of crazy whirly-gigs in front of the shrubs. There were wooden rocking chairs in different crazy colors under Japanese lanterns on the front porch. And if that wasn't enough, pink plastic flamingos stood on wire legs in the middle of the little front lawn. At the end of the drive was a brightly painted sign that read Southern Style Salon. It had big magnolia blossoms painted at each end of the lettering. The small garage had been converted to accommodate her business. A large neon comb and scissors glowed in the front window.

"I wasn't aware that a carnival had closed down in this area," Luca mumbled.

Arnold came from around the side of the house with a clipboard resting on his injured arm. The heavily mustached, middle-aged man studied his notes as he chewed on the end of his pencil. "The place is in pretty good shape, Mr. Wolff. I'll need to replace a couple of shingles and trim up that oak tree. The biggest thing is getting better ventilation in the…um…salon. I'd love to take a crack at the landscaping, with Miss Sullivan's permission of course."

Mrs. Washington came across the front lawn. She was a large, imposing woman in her early sixties. "This kitchen just will not do. There's no pantry space, and the appliances are minuscule. I'll have to bring the meals from the house each day. If you like, I can pick up the laundry then."

"Sir," Nelson called as he came down the porch steps. He was a tall, thin man about the same age as Mrs. Washington. Luca suspected that he died his hair that glossy black color. "I've put away your clothes in the room that Miss Sullivan indicated. The closet is small, and so I placed your suitcases under the bed. However, there's no work space for you in there. If we remove that overstuffed chair, I could arrange for a desk to be delivered."

"Hold on just a minute," Joy demanded. "That was my mother's chair."

Nelson bowed to her. "I'd be happy to have it safely stored for you, ma'am. It would be returned as soon as Mr. Wolff moves back to his own house."

"Well, okay," Joy conceded, "but I can't afford new ventilation."

Arnold said, "No problem, ma'am. I already have everything I'll need for the job." As he turned away, he gave Luca a sly wink. Luca knew he'd be paying for the materials for the job, but Arnold seemed to think it was necessary.

Joy turned to Mrs. Washington. "There's no need for you to bother here. I've been cooking and washing clothes since I was twelve years old."

As Luca saw the older woman's eyes widen, he chuckled to himself. No one questioned her decisions. "The name is Mrs. Washington, ma'am. I insist on helping out. I'm sure you're very capable, but you have two more people to concern yourself with and a business to run. Besides that," she dropped her voice, "Mr. Wolff can be very particular about his wardrobe."

"Then let's make a compromise," Joy said. "I'll wash my clothes and Eric's. You can see to Mr. Wolff. Also, I'll take care of breakfasts and lunches. You can bring over dinners, except on Sundays. I close the shop on Sundays, and I like to relax by cooking."

Mrs. Washington crossed her arms over her abundant breasts. "I take care of Master Eric's clothes and take Wednesdays off as well."

Joy offered her hand. "Deal. You can start

65

tomorrow."

Luca was relieved when the two women struck a happy medium without bloodshed. He went into the living room to find Eric.

Slipcovers on furniture always made him nervous. He tended to obsess over what might be hidden beneath them. Other than that, the little sitting room seemed clean and orderly. That is until he took a deep breath. He turned to Eric and whispered, "What is that horrid odor?"

Eric suppressed a laugh. "Hair gunk."

Luca nodded. "Probably the reason for more ventilation." As he continued to look around, he decided to think of the tiny house as a vacation cottage. The décor would have been perfect in the 1950's, especially the black and white kitchen. The only color in the room was the red vinyl dinette and gingham curtains. Also, floral ceramic canisters with a matching cookie jar and a large bowl of fruit sat on the counter. He noticed that Joy had returned inside and was gazing out the kitchen window.

"Eric, they're predicting rain for tonight. I was wondering if you'd mind putting the lawn mower in the shed for me."

"Sure, Aunt Joy," Eric said on his way out the back door.

She turned to Luca. "Are we waiting for Eric's entourage to show up with his belongings?"

"I'm afraid not," Luca replied. As he snatched a few ginger snaps from the cookie jar, he told her about his father having David and Melissa's house cleaned out and closed.

"Why are your family such horrible people?"

"Don't judge all of us. After all, Eric is a Wolff, too. And we have to live together for the next two months."

"Does Eric know his house was cleaned out and all of his belongings are gone?"

"No. I'd appreciate it if you'd let me tell him. We're used to overbearing people like my father. It may embarrass him for you to know how little they think of him."

"Okay, but I still think it's deplorable." She glanced out the window again. "I don't think Eric's too worried about anything right now though."

"Why do you say that?"

"My neighbors have a daughter who is just Eric's age. She likes to swim in their pool in the evenings."

One of Luca's brows rose. "It's not going to rain tonight, is it?"

Joy smiled. "I doubt it."

****

Eric was feeling pretty awesome by the time he'd finished a quick shower and tugged on new clothes. The three of them had spent the evening together. It was weird. Nothing like he was used to. To put it in one word—it was casual.

He had just stretched out on a hammock in the backyard and lit a cigarette when someone opened the back door and called his name.

"Over here," he said, releasing a plume of smoke.

"Did you forget something?" Luca held out a writing tablet and pen. "You may as well get started on the journal the judge ordered. Don't let it stress you out. A page or two each night would probably be enough."

"I doubt I'll have anything to say that anybody will

want to read. Besides that, my handwriting isn't very good. I sure wish I had my computer."

"I remember thinking the same thing when I wrote my first book."

Eric took another draw from his cigarette. "You wrote your first book with pen and paper?"

Luca tossed the pen and pad on the hammock and put his hands in his pockets. "I wrote it under a tank in the desert. The sun was too hot to be outside during the day. Believe it or not, writing is pretty good therapy for whatever bothers you."

"What had been bothering you at the time?"

Luca didn't want to think about those days. They were often the stuff of nightmares. "The same thing that bothers everybody, I guess. Trying to figure out how to survive."

"It must've been tough, being in the war."

Luca sincerely hoped Eric would never have to find out. "About as tough as quitting smoking, but I got through it and so can you." Luca snatched the pack off Eric's chest and crushed them in one hand, then pocketed the lighter. "Never get into anything that you can't control. Smoking controls you. Besides that, it makes you smell like shit. The best women don't like it."

Eric flicked the butt of his spent cigarette into the grass and watched his uncle walk away. Then he started his first journal entry.

To whom it may concern,

It's been some crazy couple days. I got out of juvie and went to court. Believe it or not, the judge was a pretty cool guy. I think he liked me, too. (When you read this, Judge-Your-Honor-sir, don't let it go to your head.)

I'm staying with my Aunt Joy and Uncle Luca. We're all living in one house. They don't really like each other, so it's kind of awkward. I figure it won't take long before they don't like me either though. Then everything will hit the skids.

For now, I have a tiny little bedroom not much bigger than a jail cell. The bed is about that small, too. It's empty cause my grandfather threw all my stuff out. Uncle Luca says he'll buy me new clothes this week. I hope I get to keep them once this is over. Back to the room though. It doesn't even have a picture on the wall. Aunt Joy says she made it that way on purpose. She says I can do whatever I want with it. I've never lived in a room that wasn't done up by a decorator. I said maybe I'd paint the walls blood red. Aunt Joy didn't even blink an eye. She said to do whatever would make me happy. I was only kidding about the red paint, but I didn't tell her that. Aunt Joy is nice no matter what my dad said.

I like her. She let us order Chinese take-out for dinner tonight. I never did that before. I also got to pick a movie to watch. I picked Ninja Assassin. Aunt Joy made popcorn, but then she fell asleep about halfway through. Uncle Luca laughed at the fight scenes. He probably knows how it's really done. He liked the movie anyway.

This afternoon I saw a girl next door. She was about my age and no bigger than me. She had crazy red hair. Beautiful! I wonder if she'll be going to the same school as me. It doesn't really matter. I'll be invisible to her, just like I am to everybody. Still, it's nice to see her. Especially when she's swimming.

Sandra Dailey

That's all for tonight.
Eric Wolff—signing off.

Chapter Ten

Friday, August 17—Life with Joy

Joy was in the middle of her typical Friday morning. As she rolled Mrs. Simons's hair, the bell above the door jingled. They both looked into the mirror to see Mrs. Carson walk in. A loud humph came from each of the older women. This had always been their way. Neither woman would think of wasting a kind word on the other.

They were both longtime residents of Summer Springs and had been widows for so long, no one could remember their husbands. For years they'd had a slow simmering feud of which no one knew the origin. The only thing people were sure of was that it had something to do with a man.

In appearance, they could have been sisters. Both women were short, skinny, white-haired and grouchy. The only way Joy could distinguish between the two was that Mabel Simons wore glasses that covered half of her face and Clara Carson carried her Chihuahua, Chester, in a knitted satchel over her shoulder. Chester who was probably older than Eric was as scrawny as his owner and shook a lot. It was the rumor there'd been several Chesters over the years, all nearly identical. Joy was reasonably sure this the only Chester she'd met.

"Isn't there some kind of health code or something to keep that dog out of here?" Mrs. Simons groused. "I don't want to carry any fleas home to my two precious kitty cats."

Mrs. Carson's face turned crimson. "I can guarantee you that Chester is at least as clean as you are. Furthermore, cats are evil."

Joy had always wondered why these two old enemies seemed to show up in the same places. Did they watch each other's movements through a telescope? Did the paperboy sell information?

"Since we don't serve food here, Mrs. Simons, there's no reason to keep Chester out. He's always behaved himself. But Mrs. Carson, you know that I can't drape you with Chester on your lap. He'll have to go into the corner." Joy made a point to put a towel and a small bowl of water in the corner when Chester came around.

"I noticed that fancy little red sports car out in the drive." Mrs. Carson made herself comfortable in a waiting chair. "I thought you might have a new customer."

Mrs. Simons rolled her eyes. "Now don't pretend that you don't know about Joy's house guests. It's the talk of the town. You're just digging for more information."

"Am not," Mrs. Carson declared. "I just didn't want to presume. You know I'm not one for the gossip mill."

The other woman huffed. "Clara, you have your nose in more people's business than the New York Stock Exchange."

"Well, I never!"

Mrs. Simons chuckled. "We both know that's a lie, you old crow."

Mrs. Carson sniffed and ignoring her sworn enemy, directed her next comment to Joy. "My dear, what are you going to do with an unruly teenage boy? You can barely take care of yourself. Do you have any idea how much those creatures eat?"

Joy gasped. "Mrs. Carson, all Eric needs is a little understanding and a lot of love. That's all any child needs. And I'll have you know that I do just fine for myself. I don't owe anyone money, and I pay my bills on time."

Mrs. Simons smirked. "I guess she told you, you old busybody."

Mrs. Carson began leafing through a magazine. "Well, be that as it may, I don't think it's proper to have a man living in your house. What are people going to say?"

Joy felt the sting of knowing that she was, once again, the talk of the town. "Probably nothing worse than they already say. Some people around here have smutty minds."

Mrs. Simons chuckled. "Clara knows all about smutty matters."

When Mrs. Carson quickly rose, a full tray of metal hair clips, combs, and scissors fell to the floor with a loud crash. "How dare you!"

On the other side of the interior door, Luca had apparently heard the racket. He threw the door open in time to have Chester run into the kitchen between his feet. The poor little dog was clothes-lined by his computer's electrical cord. Thankfully, he wasn't big enough to cause the machine to fall. Luca grabbed Chester by the scruff and held him up, so they were face to snout.

"What the hell…," Luca shouted. Nervous little Chester relieved his bladder down the front of Luca's white oxford shirt.

"What are you doing?" Joy shouted.

"I was trying to get some work done in the kitchen. The neighbor's lawn mower is so loud by my bedroom window, I couldn't hear myself think. Then, I thought a bomb had gone off in here. I came to look, but this thing ran inside. What is it—a rat?"

"It's my little Chester," Mrs. Carson cried. "Give him to me, you horrible man."

"I recommend you keep him in a bucket. He has a leak." Luca handed over the shivering pup and slammed the door behind him.

"He's a real looker, isn't he?" Mrs. Simons remarked.

****

Luca was still steaming mad when Mrs. Washington arrived for her laundry pickup, besides dropping off dinner, which she did every day except Wednesday and Sunday. After he'd told her what had happened to the wet shirt he had changed out of and put in the laundry, he continued to complain. "I don't know how a person could live this way. The sheets and towels are old and frayed. You'll have to bring some from the house. And she still has dial-up internet service. How am I going to work with that for the next two months? I have a deadline to meet. I'll have to rely on my cell phone for all my internet research and emails.

"Do you know what she has for music here? An

old console system that only plays vinyl records. The thing must be close to a hundred years old, as are most of her records. You know how much I like to listen to my music while I'm working. I have to use my phone for that as well.

"This house is so small, I run into myself coming and going. You should see the three of us huddled on her lumpy sofa around that television of hers. It looks like a hat box sat sideways. I haven't been so uncomfortable since I was deployed with the Marine Corps. Why would anyone want to live this way?"

Mrs. Washington took a deep breath. "Luca Wolff, if you weren't my boss, I'd slap your face."

Luca looked as though she'd actually done it. He melted down to sit on the edge of his bed when he saw the anger in her eyes.

His housekeeper put her fists on her hips and leaned toward him. "That poor girl has never had a break in her life, but she's still as sweet as a honeycomb. She doesn't ask anyone for anything, and she does the best she can with what she's got. She works her fingers to the bone for little cash and no appreciation. The only thing that the child has is her dignity. If you take that away from her...I swear I'll leave this house and never return."

Luca swallowed the lump in his throat. He'd never seen a hint of a tear in Mrs. Washington's eyes, but they were shining now. "I didn't realize you were so familiar with her."

"I'd never seen her until the day you moved in. Since then I've had a chance to take a look around this house. I want to show you something."

The big woman turned and headed down the short

hallway. Luca knew he'd better follow. She led him through the kitchen to a little room by the back door. He'd assumed it was a closet, but inside were old laundry appliances. On top of one machine was a neatly folded blanket and pillow. On the other was a basket of assorted clothes. Along the side wall was a wooden dowel that held a few more clothes on hangers. Beneath those was a pair of sandals and a pair of sneakers.

Luca scratched his head. "You wanted to show me her laundry?"

Mrs. Washington looked exasperated. "You just don't have a clue, do you? This is where she's keeping her things. How many bedrooms did you think this house has?"

Luca looked inside the closet-sized room again. "Where does she sleep?"

Mrs. Washington smoothed her hand over the pillow and blanket. "It's my guess these go on that lumpy little sofa at night. Do you want to tell me again about how uncomfortable you are? She's seeing to your needs before her own. And let me tell you another thing. I've done a little shopping in the stores around here. These people don't talk about her any nicer than your high and mighty family did. So, if I seem a little too friendly with her—if I seem defensive of her—I'd be proud of it."

Luca slid his hands into his pockets and shook his head. "What can I do?"

"Be appreciative and pleasant. Do what you can to make the situation easier. Help the girl out without stomping on her pride."

He felt like an ass. He'd thrown away so much more than Joy ever had. And what had he contributed besides a little money? He was behaving exactly like his dad and brother. The evidence was all around him, and he hadn't even noticed. Shame ate at his gut. "I could use a little exercise, and it looks like we have a nice breeze outside. I think I'll mow the lawn."

He'd helped his father's groundskeeper when he was a teenager. It had been a punishment, but he'd discovered he enjoyed the work. Also, he wanted to show Joy that he was willing to pitch in on his own.

Mrs. Washington dabbed at her eyes. "It wouldn't hurt you any."

Luca bounded out the door and down the back steps. He opened the shed to find an old-fashioned three blade push mower. He'd only seen an antique like it in pictures. Did the fun never end around here?

Chapter Eleven

Saturday, August 18—The Real Luca

Joy opened the shop at noon on Saturdays so she could make a nice breakfast to start the weekend. To celebrate, she slid a pan of blueberry muffins out of the oven when she heard the tap of Luca's Italian loafers on the tile floor behind her. When was the last time she'd slept until ten? Not since Melissa was still at home. It's funny how her good memories always revolved around her sister.

He walked into the room, stretching and yawning. "Is Eric still sleeping?"

"No. He's been up for about two hours. He's currently tossing a tennis ball against the back of the shop. I think he's trying to get Janet's attention."

He leaned over her shoulder. "Janet must be the girl next door."

"Yep." He smelled so good Joy couldn't help taking a big discreet sniff.

"Those muffins smell fantastic, but do I also detect the aroma of sausage and eggs?"

"You do." She pulled her apron off and hung it from a nearby hook. "I'll call Eric inside while you pour us each a cup of coffee. I like mine with cream. The cups are in the cabinet over the percolator." She had to smile at the dumbstruck look on Luca's face. Had it been that long since he'd gotten a cup of coffee for himself?

Luca scratched his head. "What exactly is a percolator?"

"It's the pot that coffee is made in, right in front of you. Just point the spout at the cup and tip it."

"I've poured coffee before," he grumbled. When he filled the first cup his eyes widened. "My God, that smells better than the muffins."

If he liked her coffee that much, she couldn't wait for his next reaction.

"It's about time we got some food around here." Eric announced as he sat at the fifties style dinette. "You've got to get up earlier, Uncle Luca. Aunt Joy said we had to wait until you were here to have breakfast. It's been hours. I'm a growing boy, you know."

She held in a laugh when Luca stared speechlessly at Eric's freshly clipped hair. Joy had trimmed it as short as Luca's around the bottom but left the top stylishly longer and off to one side. It had been the first thing he'd asked for when he woke up that morning, despite what he said about breakfast.

"I hope you don't mind that I trimmed Eric's hair without consulting you."

"Mind?" Luca shook his head. "No, I don't mind. It looks great."

Eric bounced a hot muffins from hand to hand. "I was thinking about that shopping trip for new clothes today. I figured, since I'm starting with all new gear— in a new place—around new people, I might like to change my image."

Joy was delighted. After only two days she could see a change in his attitude. She wanted to think he was happy being with them, but how much had a certain little red-headed girl influenced his mood?

She had to admit she was a little jealous of their plans for the day. She didn't want to go shopping. She couldn't afford to buy anything if she did. She had to stay here and work if the bills were going to get paid. However, Joy envied Luca the time he had to bond with Eric.

Luca's time was always more flexible. Aside from a few scheduled meetings he seemed to work when he wanted and for as long as he wanted. She'd mostly seen him at his computer when Eric was sleeping, or busy doing something on his own.

He knew what boys liked to do, and they shared a lot of common interests. She'd heard them talking about movies coming out soon, game systems that had just been developed, and court-side tickets for their favorite basketball team. The list went on and on. She didn't know about this stuff—and if she did, she wouldn't be able to afford any part of it. How could she compete?

"The shop will be closed tomorrow," she reminded Eric. "Don't forget to buy a pair of swim trunks so we can go to the beach. I know the perfect place near Saint Augustine. There's a fabulous taco truck nearby where we can have lunch. It'll give me a chance to give you your first lesson on using the public bus system."

Luca grabbed a muffin from the basket she placed on the table. "I wish I could go, but I need some time to myself. I have work to get done. My editor is screaming for the next three chapters. But a public bus?" He winkled his nose. "Those things can be dirty and filled with unsavory people. Don't you drive?"

Joy blushed. "Of course, I drive. I just don't have a car. Mine was smashed by a tree in last year's hurricane. You might say I was a little under-insured."

"Then I'll have Nelson drive you, or you can take my car."

Eric bounced with excitement. "We can take your car—the red one—are you serious?"

Joy pictured the vintage sports car Luca owned—cherry red with white side panels, white interior and a removable hard top. It was a classic in perfect condition.

"I can't drive your car!" Joy pictured the little two-seater car crushed like an accordion with her behind the wheel. She couldn't imagine how much it must be worth.

"I'll drive it," Eric offered. "My dad's chauffeur taught me how to drive on the service roads around the estate. I've never been on the open road, but I'm confident."

"No way in the world!" Luca pointed a finger at him. "You won't drive again until you have your learners permit. And even then, it won't be in my car. No one under the age of twenty-five will be driving that car."

Joy shook her head vigorously. "And I'm not driving it, either. I'd take the bus to the beach even if I still had my own car. Parking is a nightmare over there. If you do find a place, there are people who make a living by breaking into vehicles while the owners are distracted down by the water. It happens all day long."

"I see what you mean. Either Nelson can drive you

or I'll pay for a cab—your choice."

"You're getting a little high-handed, aren't you, Mr. Wolff?"

"Yes, I am. When it comes to Eric's safety, I have a right to do that. I'm also going to send my cell phone with you so you can call Nelson when you're finished or, God forbid, you have an emergency. Eric can keep it in an airtight bag inside his trunks. Maybe I'll have enough time to get him his own phone today."

Dammit, how could she argue with that?

"Nelson then. At least that way I wouldn't feel like I'm taking money from you."

"Oh, but you *will* take money from me." Luca pulled a full money clip from his pocket and pealed ten fifty-dollar bills from the top of the stack. "I can't live here for free. Don't argue about it. I spend a lot more for a hotel when I travel. Your utilities and food bill are going to go up with me and our ravenous nephew in the house."

Joy's eyes nearly jumped out of her head when she looked down at five hundred dollars sitting on the Formica table top. It was too much. She wanted to refuse it, but she couldn't. She picked off the top bill and held it out to him. "Do you have change for a fifty? The taco truck doesn't take anything larger than a twenty."

****

Luca was proud of how Eric looked in well-fitting jeans and a red and white striped soccer shirt. Eric was lying on the sofa, playing a game on his new phone when Joy finished her work day and joined them. Luca was a little curious about the strange look on her face when she noticed what Eric was doing. She probably wasn't up on the latest technology in smart phones.

"Now that we're all together," Joy announced, "I think we should talk about what Eric's responsibilities will be."

Luca and Eric looked at each other with curious expressions.

"Pardon me?" Luca asked.

Joy sat beside Eric, but looked in Luca's direction. "I appreciate you buying Eric's clothes. And the cell phone is a nice gift, but I'm sure Eric is going to want spending money. If he's to have an allowance, he'll need to work for it."

Luca was as stunned as Eric appeared. "I can afford Eric's expenses."

Eric jumped in to add, "Yeah, and I've got a whole great big trust fund,"

Joy patted Eric's hand. "That trust fund is for your future, Eric. You'll want to think for a long time about how you want to use that money. When my mother died, she left me this house. I could have sold it to start my business in a real shop, but then I would have had rent to pay somewhere. I could have sold it to buy a nicer house, but then I would have had to work for someone else to pay a mortgage. You have to weigh your options. Your Uncle Luca can probably help you with that when the time comes. He's got more experience with that sort of thing."

Then she turned to Luca. "I appreciate your willingness to pay Eric's allowance. I'm sure you know that I can't really afford it right now. But I'm also sure that Eric wouldn't want to be taken care of. He's nearly a man, and he'll want to work for his money, the same as any other man."

Luca looked across the table at his nephew. The boy looked like he'd just opened a book on quantum physics. He had to stifle a laugh. They'd just been played, and Joy was good at the game. "What did you have in mind?"

Joy folded her hands and straightened her back, clearly settling into business mode. "Well, the trash should be taken out every night, and it has to go out to the street every Tuesday morning. His room should be kept in order at all times. And he should take his turn with the dishes and the lawn work."

"That's a lot of work for a boy his age."

"Not for the boys around here. Besides that, I'm not finished."

Luca stifled a laugh. "Please, continue."

Joy did continue. "All of his homework assignments have to be handed in on time. I think it would be fair to expect him to read every day for at least as much time as he watches television and plays video games. And, of course, his grades should never drop below a 3.0."

Eric appeared to be in shock. Luca was having a hard time hiding his amusement. "Is there anything else, Sergeant Sullivan?"

Joy smiled sweetly. "No, that's all for me. Is there anything you think we should add?"

"No, I'm good."

"Wait a minute," Eric whined, "I can't do all that."

Joy patted her nephew's hand. "Eric, dear, I'm always willing to negotiate. What on that little list are you not capable of doing?"

"You don't have to put it like that." Eric pouted as he slid out of his chair.

Luca hated to see the conversation come to an end. "Where are you going?"

Eric turned with a frown. "I figure I'd better get started on those dishes and get the garbage out. I've got a lot of reading to do."

After a few minutes, Luca went to the kitchen to refill his coffee cup. Eric was elbow deep in dishwater and looked like a puppy that had just seen the business end of a rolled-up newspaper.

"What's the problem, kid?"

"I really thought Aunt Joy liked me. Now I think she doesn't want me to pick her."

Luca patted his shoulders. "I think she just did a great thing. Your aunt made you a working part of this household. She trusts you with a lot of responsibility. Hell, she even thinks you're a smart guy. Maybe she has more faith in you than you have. You need to understand something that I just learned recently. We Wolff's are used to being in a family of takers. Your Aunt Joy is a giver. It's time for you to decide which of those things you want to be?"

"I don't want to be a slave."

"If it makes you feel any better, I plan to take my turn helping out around here too. It's the least we can do. She bakes the cookies."

"She does make awesome cookies," Eric admitted.

Being reminded that he could do more for Joy, Luca went to his room and grabbed a book from his makeshift desk. Inside he wrote an inscription.

For Joy, a gracious hostess and expert cookie baker. From your house guest, JLW.

He wordlessly handed it to Joy when he returned to the living room. It was always awkward for him to gift one of his own books.

"Oh my God, a JL Wolf book!" Joy flipped the book over to see his picture on the back cover. "You're him! You're famous. I've heard a lot of people talk about your books, but I've never read one."

"You don't like my books?"

"No, I mean...I don't know. I like to read, but yours have never made it to the second-hand book store. I guess that means they're really good."

Luca laughed. "Either that, or the readers are burning them.

"This one is special. It's an advanced copy. It won't be released to the public for three more months. I'd appreciate it if you'd hang on to it until then."

"Oh, I'll keep it forever. I can't wait to read it." She took her attention away from the pages long enough to ask, "I can understand taking an F off your last name, but what does the JL stand for?"

"My real name is Jean-Luca, spelled the Italian way. My father hated it. He said the spelling was too feminine and he didn't like the name Jon, as it was too common in his opinion."

"That's silly. It's a fine name." Joy started to walk away and then changed her mind. "Do you really like my cookies?"

"I wrote that, hoping you wouldn't be mad when you discovered I'd polished off you gingersnaps."

"I was planning to make more cookies tomorrow anyway."

"Good." He grinned. "I'm partial to chocolate chip."

"And you're not still mad about what happened yesterday?"

"Not your fault," Luca assured her. "But you do need to tell those ladies to control themselves in your place of business. As far as Chester…well, hell, life must be tough for the little runt. Peeing on people is probably his only means of defense. He's forgiven."

"How about a rewind here," Eric said from the doorway. "I heard something about it being okay for little runts to pee on people. Did they teach you that in the Marine Corps, Uncle Luca?"

Luca did laugh this time. "When backed into a corner, use whatever you've got, kid."

Chapter Twelve

Friday, August 24—The First Visit

Luca sat in his car, trying to will away the onset of a major migraine. He'd waited all week for a meeting with the headmaster of West Glen Academy. The meeting hadn't gone well. For shit's sake, it was a complete disaster. The headmaster had refused to reinstate Eric's enrollment. This was Luca's first big attempt at parenting. He felt like a failure straight out of the gate.

No, he wasn't on board with the way his father and brother did things. However, there were generations of Wolffs before them who set up the family for success. They'd all started with a good education from the academy. It was a family tradition.

What would Eric's future look like? And what about his kids? The right education was imperative.

Joy didn't understand these things. All she knew was suburban mediocrity. She didn't even try to make her life better. It's all she expected for Eric as well. He couldn't let that happen. At Eric's age, they were almost at the eleventh hour to turn his life around.

Trying to play nice with Joy all week was wearing on Luca's nerves. He'd snapped at every member of his personal staff and even told his editor to kiss his ass when the man suggested a change to his manuscript. The poor guy hadn't insisted, and the difference would be a good one. Luca was too much on edge. He'd bitten his tongue so many times with Joy it was getting ragged around the edges. Their parenting styles were nearly opposite.

He agreed Eric should learn responsibility, but making him do menial chores around the house wasn't preparing him for the future...unless his future would be menial. Why hadn't she discussed it with him before she'd made her big proclamation? And, yes, he liked the way she'd cut Eric's hair, but again, she'd done it on her own, without his input. He felt like she was pushing him away from Eric.

What had happened today wasn't Joy's fault, but it was just one more thing he had no control over. He hated not being in control.

As soon as he walked through the door, the smell of chemicals nearly drove him back outside. The odor was so strong it made his eyes water. He couldn't take anymore.

Luca yelled louder than he'd intended. "How can you live with the constant stench in this house?"

Joy walked in through the kitchen door carrying a squeeze bottle of mustard. "I'm sorry. Mrs. Erving needed a perm today." She held up the bottle. "I was just making lunch. Would you like a ham and cheese sandwich?"

"No thanks," he snarled. "All I'd be able to taste is that nasty smell."

Joy narrowed her eyes. "How can you taste a smell?"

"You'd know if your olfactory receptors weren't

burned away. That stuff has got to cause brain damage."

She slammed the bottle down on the side table and put her hands on her hips. "Do you plan to claim it as a way to get Eric away from me? I wouldn't put anything past a Wolff."

"You don't know anything about me or my family. For that matter, you don't know anything about keeping a safe home environment for a child. Maybe it's something I should look into."

Joy balled her fists. "I don't know what has your panties in a bunch, but jumping down my throat isn't going to get you anything but a punch in the nose."

"Thanks for threatening physical violence. I'll be sure to mention that to my lawyer as well."

When a tap sounded on the front screen door, they both turned to see an overweight, middle-aged man looking back at them. He had a thick head of salt and pepper hair and wore a yellow short-sleeved dress shirt with brown polyester pants. In his hand was a clipboard holding a sheaf of papers curling at the edges.

Luca growled. "If you're a salesman, you've come to the wrong house today."

"My name is Larry Meyers." The man held up an identification card on the front of his wallet. At the top, it read Duval County Child and Family Services. "Is this the present home of Eric Wolff, and are the two of you his current guardians?"

Joy let Eric's social worker through the door. While his back was to her, she sent a sneer Luca's way. "Oh! Mr. Meyers, it's so nice to meet you finally. I just came in for lunch. Can I get you a sandwich and something cold to drink?"

The man rubbed his belly. "I just had my lunch, but if you have anything diet to drink…"

"I have sugar-free tea in the fridge," Joy said. "Would you like a sweetener?"

"Tea with sweetener would be great." Mr. Meyers watched Joy hurry into the kitchen then turned to Luca.

Luca felt like a heel. How long had Meyers been standing outside? "I guess you heard the disagreement we were just having. I'm very sorry. I'm not usually so short-tempered."

Meyers had a good-natured laugh. "I'm just relieved not to be on the receiving end of it. This job can get a little dicey sometimes."

Besides looking a little sloppy, Meyers had the worst breath Luca had ever encountered. He thought about offering the man a mint but decided to move to the other side of the living room.

"I've heard stories," Joy commented as she entered with a tall, icy glass of tea. "It takes guts to involve yourself in people's family matters. However, Luca and I will take any help we can get to make this situation work out for Eric. I hate to waste your time today, though. He went to the hardware store with Mr. Wolff's handyman. I don't know when to expect them back."

"That's not a problem." Meyers stirred a packet of sweetener into his drink. "I mainly wanted to meet the two of you. We'll be working together on Eric's behalf. Since he moved in so recently, I wanted to make sure he's been registered in school. It starts on Monday, you know."

"To be honest, sir, that's what has put me in such a foul mood today. I've just returned from West Glen Academy. That's the school where Eric attended last year. They've refused to allow him back due to a few problems in the past."

Joy pinned Luca with a broad, insincere smile. "Can't you have your daddy fix that for you?"

"Umm, no." Luca decided to be upfront with the truth. It would come out sooner or later anyway. "My father heads the board of trustees at West Glen. The men in our family have attended WG for generations. It seems he was the one to encourage the school to expel Eric permanently. He doesn't feel my nephew represents the family in a good light."

"In other words," Joy added, "his great-grandfather had him thrown out because he'd acted like a teenager and caused the Wolff family a little embarrassment."

"Yes," Luca admitted between clenched teeth. "I haven't had time to make inquiries at other schools."

Meyers sat his clipboard aside. "This is Friday afternoon, Mr. Wolff. It seems your time is up. Summer Springs High School is very nice. Many of the graduating class received scholarships to top universities last year. Also, a lot of renovations were made to the facility over the summer. Monday will be soon enough to get the paperwork done, and he can start by Tuesday." Meyers took a minute to scribble a note on the papers when he picked them back up. "Are there any questions I can answer for you, as long as I'm here?"

****

Joy closed the door behind Mr. Meyers before rounding on Luca. She stood in the center of the living room. "Do you know how bad that could have been?" When she gestured toward the door her hands were shaking. "If he ever even hears that we've argued like that again, we could both lose Eric. Do you want to act like your father and give up on him, just because he isn't wearing the same stupid school tie all the Wolff men wore? What was so fantastic about West Glen Academy anyway? Are the desks made of mahogany? Do they serve filet mignon for lunch on Wednesdays? Is the faculty made up of fashion models?"

Luca rolled his eyes as he stepped closer. "It's tradition. My father and uncles, my grandfather and great-uncles are all West Glen graduates. I was proud to follow in their footsteps. I wouldn't be the man I am now if it hadn't been for that school."

"How do you know? Have you ever thought about that?" Joy took a step back but didn't relent. "How do you know you wouldn't have been the president of the United States right now if you'd gone to a different school? How many presidents have come out of your alma mater?"

"You're being ridiculous." Luca folded his arms. "I never said I wanted to be president."

"Why?" She threw her hands into the air. "Is that job beneath a Wolff? After all, no one thinks more highly of your family than your family does. The rest of us see all of you as a bunch of pompous asses. Tell me one single great thing anyone in your family has accomplished in the last fifty years. Make it really magnanimous—something that others benefited from."

Luca's headache returned with a vengeance. He closed his eyes and messaged his temples. "I fought for my country. I had the backs of every man in my command. I did my damnedest to make sure they came home safely."

"Okay," Joy conceded. "But how many of those

men came from West Glen Academy and how many were the product of a public-school education? Then tell me who in your fabulous family was there to shed a tear when you shipped out? Who among the Wolffs welcomed you home and told you how proud they were of you?"

By the angry look on Luca's face, Joy could tell she'd hit a nerve. He lunged toward her without touching her. "Why don't we give it a rest and talk about your family for a while?" His voice raised a few decibels. "I only knew your sister. She hit the jackpot when she married David. Did that make you and your mother proud? According to David, it wasn't enough for Melissa. Everything he gave her was never enough. The only things I know about your mother is what the whole town had to say. It must have been confusing to have so many uncles. I guess that's why your father had to get out of the way. But he wasn't your father, was he? Does anyone know who was?"

"How dare you." Joy instinctively slapped Luca's face, instantly regretting it. She'd never struck another person in her life.

Luca's fists clenched by his sides—his eyes narrowed. "I dare the same way you do, Joy. Don't take a shot unless you're ready for return fire."

"Both of you—stop!" Eric stood in the doorway of the kitchen. "I'd rather go to a group home than live in a war zone."

Joy instantly turned from hot to cold. "How long have you been in there?"

Eric glared at them both. "When I saw Mr. Meyers' car out front, I came in the back way. Now I wish I hadn't. I could have left with him."

94

Joy's lower lip trembled. "Don't say that, Eric. Your uncle and I don't want you to go. It's just difficult learning to live together. We barely know each other."

Eric looked away. His voice dropped to a whisper. "Yeah, well you barely know me, too."

Luca walked closer and placed a hand on his shoulder. "I'm sorry, Eric. I've had a crappy day. This is all my fault. I started it. Sometimes adults argue. Sometimes they say things they shouldn't, and it gets out of hand."

"I know how it goes, Uncle Luca. I'm kind of an expert when it comes to adults misbehaving toward each other."

Eric stormed away and closed himself in his bedroom slamming the door.

Luca was confused. "What do you suppose he meant by that?"

Joy went back to the kitchen and tossed her lunch into the trash bin. "I don't know, but I guess we should let him cool down for a while. I don't know about you, but I have to go back to work."

****

Eric lay on his bed, tossing a tennis ball against the wall and then catching it. It was a dirty, old ball someone had lost in the street. It was leaving marks on the wall. He wondered when someone would come in to yell at him to stop. No doubt they'd pitch a fit when they saw what he'd done—but he'd have a few things to say back to them.

A whole fifteen minutes went by without the result he'd expected. They were probably off doing their own thing—curling hair or pecking on a computer. They'd forgotten he existed, just like everybody else.

He sat up and reached for his phone. Who could he talk to? Why was it so hard for him to make friends? It didn't matter to him where he went to school. Kids his age were stupid everywhere. He tossed the phone down on the mattress and picked up his notebook and pen.

Hello Dr. Whatever,

I usually write at night, and it's not nighttime yet. I don't even know if I'm supposed to write anything today. I'll be turning these pages over to you in a couple hours. I hope you won't want me to talk a lot. I don't feel much like talking.

I should have known this set up was too good to be true. My aunt and uncle have been perfect up to this point. Today they showed their real feelings. They were fighting just like my mom and dad. Actually, they reminded me of my parents a lot. If my folks weren't fighting about me, they were fighting about their families. It was the same as today. All they really want to do is hurt each other.

Here's another thing that's the same. I love them both, and I hate them both. They've all said the same thing. They want what's best for me. I guess I think what's best for me is for everybody to get along. I'm so tired of yelling. Without even wanting to, I end up trying to hurt them. It's like a war of words, and I don't belong on either side. I'm always squished in the middle.

If Dad loved me, why did he always do whatever Granddad or Great-granddad said to do about me? Why didn't he ever listen and take my side? If Mom really loved me why did she always drink too much and lock herself up in her room and cry all the time? That didn't do anyone any good. I was looking forward to their divorce even though it meant having to give one of them up. They would never have shared me. I would have been a weapon they used to hurt each other. Even I'm smart enough to know that. As it turned out, there wasn't any divorce. They got killed. I guess that's my fault too. I caused all the trouble.

Before I came along, Aunt Joy and Uncle Luca didn't know each other. They didn't have any problems. They didn't know or care what was going on with me. Now, here I am, and they're fighting.

I don't know what to do. I don't have anywhere else to go. For now, I'll try to stay out of their way. I'll play the invisible man until I can come up with another plan.

Thanks for listening. At least, I'll pretend that you're listening.

Eric Wolff—over and out

Just as he put the journal and pen away for safe keeping, a voice came from the other side of his bedroom door. "Eric, can I come in?"

He wished he could say no. "Sure, Aunt Joy."

"I was wondering if you'd like me to ride the bus with you to see Dr. Johnson today."

"Uncle Luca said he'd take me in his car."

"I guess that would be a lot more fun." She looked at the marks on the wall. "Eric, I know I said you could do what you wanted to your room, but is that the look you had in mind?"

"I like it."

"Okay."

After she'd left, Eric laid back on his bed. How was he going to clean those stupid marks off the wall?

Chapter Thirteen

Saturday, August 25—The Runner

Saturday was the shortest work day of Joy's week, but today seemed to drag on forever. She was glad when her last client walked out the door.

Cutting hair was easy, but it was impossible to put back on if done incorrectly. It was a miracle she hadn't made any huge mistakes. Chemicals could burn hair…as well as skin. Styling required your full attention. Something she didn't have a lot of today. Luckily, she'd been working at her craft for so long, it came as second nature.

Her mind was occupied by thoughts of Eric. He hadn't eaten much at dinner last night and went straight to his room after his talk with Dr. Johnson. She'd hoped he'd feel better after the therapy appointment, but that didn't seem to be the case. This morning he'd been just as sullen. The purple smudges under his eyes showed her he hadn't gotten much sleep. The argument yesterday had upset him terribly. She and Luca had really screwed up.

As soon as she walked through the kitchen door, she called for Luca. He appeared from the living room as GQ as always, even though he wore a rock concert T-shirt and cargo shorts. The concerned expression on his face didn't register right away. She had an idea to lift everyone's spirits. "What do you think about taking Eric and me out tonight? We could go somewhere fun, burgers, mini-golf, go-carts…It's the last weekend before school starts. We should celebrate."

Luca pushed his hands into his pockets. "It sounds great, Joy, but Eric isn't here."

"Where did he go?"

"I don't know."

She pulled the curtains back over the sink. "What do you mean, you don't know? It's almost dark. When did he leave? Why didn't you ask where he was going? Did someone pick him up?"

Luca brought back one hand to run through his hair. "He walked outside after you went to work. I thought he was going to mow the grass or toss his ball and watch for Janet. I went to my room and spent about six hours on the computer. I realized I hadn't heard the refrigerator open in all that time, so I started looking for him."

"Six hours?" Joy grabbed her stomach to stop its flipping. "Have you called his friends? Maybe someone is having an end of summer party. He used to know the kids around here when he was younger."

Luca leaned against the counter. "I have to be honest with you. I didn't know how much I could trust him when I bought him a phone so I had it cloned to mine."

She raised a hand to stop him. "Enough of the computer jive. What does this cloning business mean? What exactly did you do, Luca?"

He took in a deep breath, and then let it out on a slow sigh. "There are ways to play with phones, connect them in a way so that one person knows what's going on with another. It's called cloning. Eric's phone is cloned to mine; I know when he's received or made calls."

"And?" she asked, impatient with all this. Eric was gone and Luca didn't know when he'd left, or how long he'd been gone.

Luca ran a hand through his hair. "He hasn't received a call or text since he got it. I don't think he has any friends. He's always playing games and watching videos on the internet, but I've never seen him contact anyone. He doesn't even use social media. Who doesn't use social media?"

"I don't." Joy felt tears welling up. Eric was more like her than she'd realized. She truly wanted him to be like Luca: happy, well-balanced, popular, and successful. Where could he have gone? "Maybe we should call the police."

"I've checked the burger joint, the pizza place, the ice cream shop, the skate park, the arcade, the library— I even went inside all the stores," Luca told her. "There's nothing the police can do."

She reached for the kitchen wall phone. "They need to put out an Amber Alert for him. He could be hurt."

Luca grabbed the phone from her hand. "Don't do that, Joy. If you call the police, they'll see his record and tag him as a runaway. They won't bother looking for him. If they do find him, they'll put him back in the system. Don't you think I've been trying to figure all this out while I drove up and down every street in town?"

"Why didn't you let me know what was going on?"

she cried. "It's not like I work miles away from here."

"I was hoping he'd be back before you found out. I knew you had appointments to take care of, and I didn't want to worry you."

Joy started pacing a six-foot section of her kitchen floor. "I've been too hard on him. He doesn't think I want him here. Has he complained to you? You can tell me. My feelings don't matter at a time like this."

Luca grabbed her shoulders to hold her still. "I seriously don't think that's the problem. You've gone out of your way to make this transition as easy as possible. I'm the one who's been too tough. My temper has made him afraid of me. He was probably too scared to spend the day alone with me."

Joy shook her head. "He looks up to you. You understand the way he's been raised. If anything, he relates to you more than he does me."

He huffed. "Yeah, we're a couple of really great people, but neither of us has gotten to know him very well. The kid is as closed up as a clam."

"How well can you expect to know anyone after barely more than a week? Especially considering that we've all been under a lot of stress. I don't know about you, but I haven't been able to come to terms with Melissa's death. What must it be like for Eric to have lost her and David both?"

Luca put an arm around her shoulder and pulled her against his chest. "I'm sorry."

"So, what do we do?"

"I don't know." Just then the phone in Luca's pocket rang.

Luca nearly fumbled his phone to the floor trying to press the answer button. Joy caught it in time. They both groaned when they saw it was Arnold's name across the top of the screen. He put it to his ear and walked toward the back door. Eric had been spending time with his handy-man on trips to the hardware store. He'd probably bonded with Eric more than either of them had. Perhaps this was another person who could join the search.

"Hi, boss. Are you somewhere on the estate?"

Luca sent a frown in Joy's direction. "No. Why would you think that?"

"I was just driving back to the house with the new fitting for your pool pump. When I passed Mr. David's old house I saw Eric there. Isn't that house emptied out?"

"Yes, it's cleaned out. What was Eric doing?"

Joy grabbed his sleeve the moment he said Eric's name.

"He was sitting out by the basketball hoop smoking a cigarette," Arnold replied. "The kid looked pretty down. I don't know if he hitched a ride or what, but he's a long way from Summer Springs by himself. Should I go over and see if he needs a ride back?"

"No. I'd appreciate it if you'd try to keep an eye on him until I get there. If he takes off again, see where he goes and give me another call. I'll be there as soon as I grab my keys."

"No problem, boss. I really like the kid, but I had a feeling he might be AWOL."

When Luca turned back around Joy was inches away with his keys dangling from one finger. "Do you mind if I handle this alone?"

She swiped away a stray tear. "As I said before, he relates to you. I'd probably just start blubbering all over him anyway."

Luca ran to Eric's room and returned carrying his new basketball. "We may need an hour or so before we head back. I'll take him to get something to eat if he's hungry. I can't imagine him going this long without food."

"I'll have fresh cookies ready. That's about all I know to do in a situation like this."

"And it's appreciated." Luca smacked a kiss on her cheek. "You're the greatest. Don't ever doubt that."

****

Twenty long minutes later, Luca spotted Eric where Arnold said he'd be. Even though the basketball court by David's house was only a half court with one light, Eric looked small sitting on a stack of grass seed bags. When he heard the door to Luca's car close, he looked up. Luca dribbled a ball as he walked toward him. "How about a game of horse?"

"I'm too scrawny to play basketball. I don't suppose you'd know what that's like."

"I wasn't any bigger than you at your age. I didn't get a growth-spurt until the summer between my sophomore and junior year."

Eric pulled a pack of cigarettes from his pocket and lit one. "So, you're telling me I have two more years to be a runt. You sure know how to lift a guy's spirit. Thanks a lot."

"That's not going to help." Luca took the cigarette from his hand and took a deep draw from it. He slowly blew the smoke out in a thin stream.

"Hey, you don't smoke."

Luca turned his head to the side to face Eric. "I haven't for the last five years. I guess you're a bad influence on me."

"That's just what I need. Guilty of one more thing. I ruin lives everywhere I go."

Luca laughed. "You haven't ruined anything…except maybe a good game of horse. You can play b-ball if you try. You just have to run faster, jump higher, and put more power behind your shots than anyone else on the team."

Eric sneered. "And I guess you were a star player when you were my size."

Luca threw the cigarette in the dirt beside the concrete court and crushed it with the toe of his shoe. "Hell, no. I never even tried out for the team. Do I look like an idiot? Those guys would have killed me. But I could have if I'd worked hard enough."

Eric started to reach for his cigarette pack again, but decided it was useless. "What's your point then?"

Luca placed a hand on Eric's shoulder. "My point is—no one is perfect. You haven't ruined anything. You've just made a few mistakes. We all have."

Eric nudged the hand away. "Then why is everything turning to shit like it did when my mom and dad were here? You and Aunt Joy hate each other just like they did. And I'm the reason you fight."

"Wow. You give yourself all the credit, don't you, Eric?"

"I've heard what you say to each other. It's true."

Luca pointed a finger at him. "First off, I don't hate your aunt. I don't believe she hates me. We're just under a lot of pressure."

"Because of me."

"Let me finish." Luca thumped Eric's earlobe. "We're both worried about losing you. We can't both keep you, but we both desperately want to. In that way, I guess you're right. We love you too much. And don't act like I'm weird for saying that. It's true."

Eric used the toe of his shoe to bury the mangled cigarette butt. "You think so?"

"I know so. She's trying so hard to make everything perfect for you—and to my surprise—she's doing the same for me. On top of that, she's wearing herself to the bone trying to handle a bunch of clients who don't appreciate her. And she's worried about money all the time. She's too proud to ask for help. I respect her for that—even if it does drive me a little crazy.

"I have an agent hounding my every waking moment as though I'm hiding a trunk full of best-selling novels in my closet. It's not easy working in a strange place with noisy neighbors and the smell of hair gunk. Dammit, you have me saying that now.

"And, while we're trying to work through all that, we have to deal with a judge with off-the-wall ideas, a caseworker with the worst breath ever, and a therapist we don't know and are not allowed to ask about."

Eric nodded. "Yeah, I can see that's tough. I guess Aunt Joy is pretty upset with me. What do you think is going to happen when I get back?"

"She'll probably stuff you full of fresh-baked cookies and cry a little."

"Girls. Dammit. I suppose I can handle that." Eric snatched the ball and headed for the car. "Last one there has to do the dishes."

"Hey, Eric!" When the boy stopped and turned toward him, Luca continued, "If you have a problem from now on, you come to me, and we talk man-to-man, right?"

Eric looked down as he dribbled the ball. "Yeah, sure."

"By the way, how did you get here from Summer Springs?"

"I teleported."

Luca wondered if their conversation had soaked in at all.

****

Hey, Doc Johnson,

I figure you're going to find out about it anyway, so I'm just going to tell you myself. I bailed for a while today. I just needed time to think, and I figured the fam could use some thinking time too. It didn't occur to me I was making stuff worse for them than it already is.

It seems like I've always been a burden to everyone—first my parents and now my guardians. Is it like that for all kids?

When I see ordinary people in stores and restaurants and stuff, they seem happy. I don't hear other kids in school talk about not being wanted at home. My parents never actually said as much, but they were always shutting me out.

I kind of felt weird when Uncle Luca found me today. Nobody ever came looking for me before. He didn't yell or anything.

I think he's pulling my chain about being small like me. He's like Thor kind of big now. That didn't happen overnight. I'd never be lucky like that.

Anyway, I wanted to let you know I didn't do anything wrong while I was gone. Nothing I'd get arrested for anyway.

See you Friday,

Eric Wolff—Prince of Summer Springs

He'd left out the part about hitch-hiking. No need to give the old folks a heart attack. Teleporting, though, that was a good one.

Chapter Fourteen

Monday, August, 27—Apologies and Doubts

Early on Monday morning, Luca found Eric at the back of the kitchen table behind a stack of blueberry pancakes. He'd spent all day yesterday making up for the way he'd starved himself the day before. The boy had a bottomless pit hidden under his shirt.

Joy stood at the stove, filling a plate for him. No matter how badly he behaved, she made sure he was well fed. He never saw her happier than when she was feeding someone. Once he was finally in his own home, he'd have to hit the gym hard. He poured himself a cup of coffee and took a seat next to Eric.

"Breakfast smells terrific."

"I hope so." Joy gave him a forced smile. "I can't guarantee I won't have to give a perm later today and ruin the atmosphere."

"About that." Luca sat down the coffee he'd just picked up. He'd been thinking about Friday's argument the whole time he'd tried to write yesterday. He'd also thought about Eric's reaction to it. "I said a few things the other day I should apologize for."

Eric glanced at his pancakes with disappointment. "Do you want me to leave the room?"

Luca gave it some thought. "No, you may as well

stay. Sometimes a person says or does things that hurt others, and you need to know it's unacceptable. The thing a man regrets most is the pain he's caused others. I was mean to Joy. I admit it."

"Really, that's not necessary. All is forgotten," Joy muttered.

He noticed she hadn't used the word *forgiven*.

He gave her a severe look. "Yes, it is necessary. I went too far with the cracks I made about your family. You hit a nerve when you reminded me about my dad's reactions to my time in the service. You were right. But no one wants to hear their family insulted. I should have realized I was doing that to you. My head wasn't in a good place."

He turned to Eric. "I've been a little lost without my brothers-in-arms. They became my second family. I avoided coming home for a long time. By doing that, I missed spending time with you. I deeply regret that the most. I feel I hurt you in a way."

Eric poked his pancake a few times with his fork. "Yeah, well, I was here. I understand, and I don't blame you for staying away."

Joy placed a fresh bottle of syrup on the table to replace the one Eric had almost emptied. "I was out of line, too. I hate the way people who've never taken the time to know me think they can judge me. I've been judging you based on the behavior of your family. That's just as bad."

Luca grasped Joy's wrist to keep her from returning to the stove. "The things I said about your father...that was uncalled for. I want you to understand how sorry I am."

"Sometimes the truth hurts. There's nothing

109

anyone can do about that."

Her smile seemed a little shaky, so Luca decided to drop the conversation until later. He turned to Eric. "Are you excited to see your new school?"

"I'm sure it's a school, like any other school." His eyes suddenly flashed with inspiration. "But how cool would I look driving up in an awesome sports car on my first day!"

"Probably cooler than you'll look *riding* up in that car, but that's what you're going to do."

"Are you ever going to let me drive your car?"

"Maybe when you get married. That should give me at least ten years to get used to the idea. I'll drive you today; after that, Nelson will take you back and forth."

"No way!" Eric whined loudly. You'd think he'd been asked to show up to school naked. "I'm going to school the same way every other kid in the neighborhood is going—on the bus."

Luca directed to Joy. "You started this bus business."

Joy dried her freshly washed hands and sat down at the table. "I think it's a great idea. It'll give him a chance to meet the other kids around here and make some friends. I bet Janet rides the bus."

"I guess you're right…but is it safe?"

She threw her head back and laughed. "Luca, you drive around in a car that's barely bigger than a skateboard. He's safer than you are."

He had to admit she was right. "Okay, you can try using the bus. However, if you run late and miss it, Nelson or I will be available to take you. There'll be no excuses for not attending classes this side of the bubonic plague."

"I get it, I get it," Eric groused. "What about lunch money?"

Luca reached into his wallet and produced a fifty-dollar-bill.

Joy snatched it from his hand before Eric could take it. "Whoa! Hold on, Mister Moneybags. Do you want him to get mugged on his first day?"

"They have muggings at this school?"

"I don't know, but I was considering taking it myself. Don't you have something smaller?"

Luca rummaged in his front pants pocket. "I think I have a twenty in here somewhere, would that do?"

"I never bought lunch at school, but I'm sure it will."

He looked at her with a raised brow. "How did you get lunch?"

"I used the brown-bag method. Have you ever heard of it?"

He shook his head. "No."

"Never mind. You wouldn't understand."

Luca made a mental note to google brown-bag method.

****

Joy only had three clients before lunch. Mondays were always disappointing. To be honest, she barely got by on what she made the whole week. Maybe she should think about working through lunch and more hours in the evenings. Would she be able to keep a more extended schedule after Luca moved back to his own house? No one would be available for Eric. She refused to think Eric would be leaving as well. Now that he was so much a part of her life, she couldn't give

111

up her one day off. Sundays were their day together.

It was kind of Luca to pay rent, but after he was gone, she'd have to find some way to increase her income. Feeding a teenage boy was no small feat. Maybe she should look into one of those work-from-home-in-your-spare-time things. They all seemed like a scam to her, though.

When Luca mentioned that he and Nelson would be available to drive Eric to school, she wished she could volunteer as well. It had been difficult not to have a car, but now it was a problem. What if she were alone with Eric when something happened to him? Cars were expensive when you added up the payments, tags, insurance, maintenance, and repairs. She just didn't believe she'd inherit Melissa's money. It was too good to be true.

Luca had come in without her noticing. "What's for lunch?"

She'd been deeply engrossed in her pity party. He dropped a stack of papers on the table and sat across from her. She pushed her plate toward him. "It's a tuna salad sandwich and chips. I lost my appetite before I touched it."

"Was it something I did?"

"No. I was just feeling sorry for myself."

He looked truly concerned. "Is there something I can help you with?"

She couldn't make her problems his. She shook her head and reached for the papers while he took a bite of her sandwich.

"I had no idea the extent of paperwork involved in putting one kid into school. It wasn't this hard getting into the Marine Corps."

Joy looked through the door to the living room. "Where is Eric?"

"He was given his class schedule and a map of the school. He's already started. He said it was better than sticking out like a sore thumb tomorrow." He pointed to the forms in her hand. "This is mostly about his medical and dental insurance. I've already called Michael Knight to set that up. He also volunteered to make appointments for Eric's check-ups."

That was another thing she hadn't considered. How was she going to manage? Eric deserved the best. Luca even had a lawyer willing to take care of these details for him. Man, was she in over her head?

Luca popped a chip into his mouth and continued. "Michael suggested I put him in the same insurance group I have for myself and my staff. If you're not happy with your own coverage, I could probably add you, also."

She hadn't had insurance since she'd aged out of her mother's policy. Her care came from the county health department. "No, I'm fine," she lied. "Would you like a glass of iced tea?"

"Sure," Luca replied. "There was something I was meaning to mention. You fell asleep before I finished my shower last night. I took the liberty of going into your salon and getting a tube of styling gel. I didn't want to drive into the city that late. How much do I owe you?"

She shrugged. "Don't worry about it. I'll just write it off."

"You can't do business by giving things away."

Joy felt a little insulted and embarrassed. "How much is that book worth that you gave me?"

He took another bite of the sandwich and stared at her as he chewed. Something was on his mind. "Speaking of doing business, I noticed the certificates you have on the wall out there."

"Yes. I'm required by law to post them in full view of my customers."

Luca nodded and continued. "Besides your business and health department papers, I noticed that you have both a cosmetology and a barber license."

"I figured I might as well cover all my bases."

"I didn't see any mention of barber work on your sign, so I looked you up on Google. There's nothing on the internet for you or your shop."

A few of her customers had mentioned the same thing. She told him the same thing she'd said to them. "I have to order some of my supplies and materials online, but that's the extent of my dealings with it."

He persisted. "You're qualified to do waxing, shaving, manicures, and pedicures. A lot of men get those things done as well as women—not to mention haircuts. You're missing out on a lot of business."

She shook her head. "Men around here wouldn't be interested. Most of them have gone to the same barber since they were children. And forget about waxing or manicuring these guys."

"Maybe this isn't the best place to set up shop."

Who was he to tell her how to run her business? "It's what I have, and it's worked for me so far. Besides that, I'd need a ton more equipment. I don't have space or the money to buy it."

"Well, what about advertising? You could double your business by placing ads in local papers and magazines. You should have a website to show what you can do. It wouldn't be hard to maintain a few social media sites as well."

Frustration was welling up and stinging her eyes. "I'm just me. I do hair for the little old ladies in Summer Springs. It's no big deal."

He wouldn't relent. "But don't you see? It could be a big deal. You'd be a lot more successful if you'd stop thinking of yourself as a poor hairdresser and start thinking of yourself as a successful business owner."

Joy's nerves were pulled like the band on a slingshot. "I can see how that would be easy for someone who had an endless supply of family money to back them up. What you don't understand is that I don't have anyone to rely on but myself. The world looks a lot different from my side of the tracks. Don't tell me how I'm selling myself short. You don't know anything about how hard I've worked to get where I am. Starting from nothing isn't easy."

"Then let me help you."

"I don't need anyone's help," she screamed.

Joy ran back to the shop and slammed the door between them. She scrubbed tears away with the back of her hand. No one ever saw her cry for herself. She'd be damned if he'd be the first.

The things he was saying did make sense. Joy knew that. But those things were out of her reach. Maybe it wouldn't have bothered her so badly if she hadn't been thinking about her financial situation before he'd sprung it on her. He hadn't meant any harm. People like him always discussed business ideas. She just wasn't one of them. She'd never be one of them. Perhaps it would be best if Eric grew up in Luca's world. He might become a more successful man.

That thought just brought on more tears. Joy didn't want to be alone anymore. Having a make-believe family had been better then she'd expected. Not only did she enjoy the youthful energy Eric provided, but she also liked having a handsome and remarkable man to share her days. The only thing still missing was someone to share her nights. But that wouldn't happen.

Joy looked in the mirror at her dark skin and wild hair. She was the product of two worlds, but she didn't belong in either one. She especially didn't belong with someone like Luca Wolff.

Chapter Fifteen

Friday, August 31—The Storm

Thunder shook the wood frame house causing the window panes to rattle. When lightning filled the room, Joy could see it was only four AM. Something was wrong. Storms didn't make her feel this anxious. They'd always made her feel rejuvenated—like nature was in the process of renewing itself. This morning something was different.

Suddenly, a muffled shout came from down the hall. She jumped from the sofa cracking her shin on the coffee table. Dammit, she hated that stupid thing.

Eric's door flew open as she reached for it. His eyes were wide and unfocused. "Something's wrong with Uncle Luca," he croaked.

"It's okay," she assured him. "Go back to bed. I'll take care of it."

For the first time in the two weeks since he'd moved in, she eased the door open to the room that used to be hers. Another flash of lightning showed Luca laying with a tangle of sheets around his hips. It was all that covered his nakedness. He was soaked in sweat. On his side facing her, he was holding his pillow tightly. His eyes were closed, but his brow was pinched in a scowl. "Incoming, incoming, take cover!"

He didn't seem panicked. His voice was insistent, urgent, commanding. He was as forceful in his dream as he was while awake. He'd been born to lead others. Had the crashes and flashes of the storm taken his subconscious back to the battlefield? How often did this happen?

She slowly approached and put her hand on his upraised shoulder. "Wake up, Luca. You're having a dream."

In an instant, she found herself lying next to him, his body half covering hers. "Take cover, soldier," he barked. "Where the hell is your helmet?"

Memories flew through her mind of the scenes she'd read in the book he'd given her. It was a book about the relationships of soldiers who worked at flushing the enemy from the homes of innocent villagers in war torn areas of Afghanistan. There'd been a disclaimer in the first few pages saying the story was a work of fiction. The names and places may have been changed, but she realized he'd actually lived through the events. That's where his inspiration had come from. Her heart ached for him.

"Cavanaugh! Has anyone seen Cavanaugh?"

He did seem panicked now. He thought one of his men was missing. "He was supposed to be on watch. Where the hell is he? I can't see Cavanaugh."

"Wake up, Luca," she soothed. "It's okay. It's only a dream."

Luca sprang to a sitting position. He ran his fingers roughly through his hair back and forth trying to force himself back to the present. He was awake now. "Damn, damn, damn, damn, damn!" Apparently, this had happened before, and he was annoyed.

"It's okay." Joy rose to wrap her arms around his back and hold him. Her thin T-shirt clung to his perspiring chest. She realized she was only wearing the old shirt with a pair of running shorts, but the room was dark. Thankfully the storm was moving away.

For several minutes they sat, their legs tangled, heads resting against each other's necks, hands exploring one another's backs, breaths slowing to normal.

"I'm sorry I woke you."

Her hand smoothed the back of his hair. "I'm sorry you had a bad dream. Is there anything I can do?"

His hands rested on her hips. He leaned back to look in her eyes. His expression was one she'd never seen before. "I don't mean to be rude, but under different circumstances, I'd toss you down on this bed and strip your clothes off. I'd pound into you like a man on a mission. Perhaps you should leave before I ignore the circumstances."

Joy studied his face. He was serious. Her entire body felt hot and liquid. She thought about staying, but they weren't even friends. She wasn't the kind of woman to sleep around. She'd only ever had two lovers. To a man like Luca Wolff, she'd just be one more conquest and not even a particularly memorable one.

She returned to the sofa but couldn't go back to sleep. It wasn't only the fact that her body ached for what Luca had suggested. She thought about what her life had been like before the last two weeks and wondered if it would ever be the same.

No matter what the judge decided, Eric would be a part of her world now. How much of a role would Luca play in that world? Would he disappear as completely as he had halfway through her sister's wedding reception?

She felt the same now as she'd felt that day when she'd caught him watching her, standing across the room looking incredibly distinguished in his Marine Corps uniform. She'd had teenage fantasies about him for months.

****

Eric sat in the last seat of the school bus with his feet on the back of the seat in front of him. His notebook rested on his raised knees.

Hi Dr. Johnson,

Greetings from the back of the school bus. I'm writing super early today because something pretty awesome happened this morning. Lucky you, no boring story about school today.

It was about four in the morning, before the butt-crack of dawn. A massive storm was going on outside. Thor was going overboard with the thunder and lightning. It would have made a bodacious laser light show, you know?

I nearly jumped to the ceiling when Uncle Luca started hollering. He was having a nightmare.

I used to have them, too, but Dad said only babies get scared. From then on, I'd stay awake all night if I thought it might happen. I didn't want anybody to think I was a baby. But now, I find out that a tough guy like Uncle Luca has bad dreams too. He's not just tough because I think he is. He was a marine—an honest to God hero.

Aunt Joy came running. She wasn't mad or laughing at him or anything. She looked really worried.

She told me to go back to bed. She probably didn't want Uncle Luca to be any more embarrassed than he was going to be, having her see him like that.

I know I should have listened to her, but I was pretty concerned myself. When she tried to wake him up, he wrestled her into the bed and thought they had people shooting at them, like when he was in Afghanistan. She finally did shake him out of it, and then they started hugging. Just sitting there hugging. That's when I figured it was over and I should go back to bed.

I've been thinking about it all morning. The two of them wrapped up together like that looked like the pictures on those sappy, lovey-dovey books girls read. It seemed like they really cared about each other. I don't remember ever seeing my parents together like that. They didn't love each other, though. Wouldn't it be awesome if Uncle Luca and Aunt Joy started loving each other? Then we'd be able to stay together, and I wouldn't have to decide between them.

I figured if I told you about it, you could help me think of ways to make them fall in love. I think it would be the best solution for all of us.

See you soon,

Eric Wolff—over and out

Eric felt a tap on his knee and looked up into the beautiful blue eyes of his red-headed neighbor. "Hey, we're at school. You're not going to stay on the bus all day, are you?"

"Umm, I guess not." Jeez, his voice sounded like Kermit-the-Frog.

The girl smiled. She was more beautiful up close than she was in her pool next door. "My name is Janet.

I was wondering if you have a spare pen I could use. I guess I must have lost mine."

"Sure." Eric handed over his only pen. He nearly knocked her over as he pushed his way down the aisle. "I'd better get to class."

He felt like such a dweeb. She probably thought he was mental.

****

Luca was in a sour mood as he drove across town. He'd had a crappy morning. He'd lost sleep because of another nightmare. It had been weeks since he'd had one. Then he woke with a half-naked Joy on his lap. The only thing that had preserved his dignity was a wadded sheet between them. He was so stunned he'd said the first thing that had come to mind. God, he was such a jerk.

He guessed it had been better than just grabbing her for a deep, sex-starved kiss. He couldn't remember the last time he'd had a date. He wasn't the kind of guy that needed a woman all the time. That was starting to change, living in such close quarters with Joy. Every time he looked around she was bending over to pick something up or stretching to reach something. She had no idea how attractive she was or the effect she had on him.

He was glad he could avoid her today but not at the expense of meeting with his brother at the club. He hated the club. His family would never refer to it as the North Links Golf and Country Club. No, they had to make it sound like their own private playground and everyone else there had been personally invited on Wolff stationary.

In the circular drive, he glared at the over-eager

parking valet. "I've inspected every inch of this car and noted the mileage. Think twice before you take it for a joy ride and don't let go of these keys."

"Don't worry, sir. My dad would kill me if I lost this job."

Luca looked down at the boy's shoes. They were worth more than this kid's job would pay in a month. His dad had to be a member. Making him work a job at all was probably a punishment. "He wouldn't be worried about your job...he'd be too busy trying to find your body."

The snarky smile disappeared from the boy's face as his head snapped back. "Yes, sir. I'll take care of it personally."

Okay, maybe that last bit was a little over the top, but he really dreaded going inside.

He would have refused when Daniel called that morning, but his brother said he wanted to discuss Eric's future. He had to keep in mind that Daniel was Eric's grandfather.

When he saw Daniel waiting at the main entrance, it occurred to Luca that his brother looked more like their old man every day. He was tallish and heavy in a cream-colored, linen suit. His silver hair had started to thin on top, letting his scalp shine through. He looked like a refrigerator. Luca thanked God once again that he'd taken after his mother.

Daniel shook his hand inside the air-conditioned lobby. It made him feel as though they were starting a business meeting. "Come into the dining room. We already have a table."

Luca followed and found out what his brother had meant by *we*. Gerald Wolff waited at his usual table in the center of the room. He was being double teamed, or as Eric would say, ganged up on.

Before he could say a word, his father flagged over a waiter. "We're finally all here. You can bring us each a porterhouse steak with an endive salad. And we'll have a round of whiskeys, neat. Oh, and make sure those steaks are medium rare, or I'll be speaking to your boss."

"You know..." Luca slowly sat across from his father. "That doesn't really work for me. I'll have a burger, medium well, with mayo, lettuce, and tomato, hold the onion. Oh, and I'll have a root beer...on the rocks."

"Would you like fries with that, sir?" The waiter's eyes sparkled. He'd probably waited for years to say that to one of these smug bastards.

Luca flipped his white linen napkin open and placed it over his leg. "Excellent suggestion, my good man."

Gerald busied himself wiping down his silverware with his own napkin. "You've barely gotten through the door, and you're already being difficult."

Daniel looked over his knife and fork for spots. "I told you this meeting would be useless, Father."

Luca already wanted to leave. "I'm a grown man. I don't need anyone to decide what I eat." He turned to Daniel. "Did you bring your own bib, or is it in Daddy's pocket?"

"Enough of that," Gerald bellowed. "We're here to discuss Eric."

"I don't know what there is to discuss," Luca responded before taking a sip of water from a crystal glass at his table setting. "You've barely been around the boy. You didn't take any responsibility for him after David died. You didn't even have the balls to tell him his parents were dead. That's cold, man. And you haven't asked about him since I've had him. As a matter of fact, you've thrown away everything the kid owned."

His brother's lip curled at the mention of Eric. "It's you who doesn't know him, Luca. He's been on his best behavior since you took him in. I'm sure he'd like to get back to the Wolff way of living. If you'd been around earlier, you'd know the child is out of control. He's perfectly capable of stealing you blind and killing you in your sleep. Even David had given up on him."

The older man's head bobbed up and down in agreement. "It's true. David was happy to let his wife take the boy after their divorce was started. I think it would be best to continue with his plan to have Eric put in a very strict boarding school in Samoa. I have the name of the place at my office. Then, Luca, you can return to globe-trotting and keep writing your little books. You'll forget about him before you get to the airport."

Their drinks arrived, giving Luca a moment to think. This was a little more than he could believe. David had fought like crazy to stay out of boarding schools. He'd never agree to send his own kid to one. "David was going to send him to Samoa—the island in the South Pacific? What the hell for?"

"It's an excellent school, Luca. And, yes, it's located in the South Pacific." His father took a drink of his whiskey. When had he started drinking hard liquor so early in the day? "It's designed for unruly teenagers. They know how to handle problems like him."

"If Eric was a problem, I can certainly see why."

Gerald continued as though he hadn't heard Luca. "The family is willing to pay for Eric's expenses and schooling as long as this is the school he attends. However, Melissa's sister will not get a dime. You must make sure she doesn't gain custody. A few payoffs here and there should help."

Luca looked at both men. Something seemed fishy. "If you are so against Eric, why don't you suggest she take him?"

Daniel sipped from his glass and grimaced. Luca hoped he had a stomach ulcer. "Surely, you're not that naïve. She's only in it for the money. She doesn't care how much Eric stains the Wolff name."

Gerald took over the conversation. "Son, I'm sure it's been very cozy living with the woman. She does have a lot to offer a man. But I'm also sure many men have been in her bed before you, and many will be there after this is over. Don't let her influence your judgment. You've been raised better than that."

Luca's phone rang. "I'm done with this." He reached in his pocket.

"A phone at the table is bad manners," Gerald complained. "Is this what you learned from being a soldier?"

"No, sir. I learned to be a man in the marines. Not a worm like you and your sidekick."

Daniel rose from his chair and threw his napkin on the table. "I don't care if you were in a war. I'll still knock you down, little brother."

Luca laughed. "Is that the best you've got? I could kill you a hundred different ways with that fork in front of you."

Gerald Wolff turned his nose up in true Wolff style. "I see you take more than your looks from your mother. You have her Italian temper as well as an unstable mind."

"Don't drag Mom into this, old man. A cold fish like you could never hope to understand a real woman."

As Luca walked to the lobby, his waiter stepped in his path. He held up a white paper bag and a tall Styrofoam cup with a straw in the top. "I had a premonition," he said with a smile. "Don't worry about the bill. I put it on Mr. Wolff's tab."

"You're a man among pigs, my friend."

Luca took his keys from the boy outside and noticed his car hadn't moved an inch since he'd left it. As he pulled onto the road, he pressed the buttons on his phone to hear the message that had been left.

"Mr. Wolff, this is Mr. Peterson. I'm the principal at Summer Springs High School. We've had a little problem with your nephew. Please come to the school as soon as possible."

Chapter Sixteen

Friday, August 31—A New Threat

Florida public schools were different than private schools. They were usually single level and broken up into several buildings connected by breezeways. The center building typically housed the offices and larger rooms, like the gymnasium, auditorium, cafeteria, or a combination of all three. They were all designed to be used as hurricane shelters when the need arose. That's where Luca headed.

No matter what kind of school you were in—one thing remained the same: the principal's office. It might be decorated in modern-manufactured or traditional wood furniture, but the atmosphere was always foreboding. Few students or parents, guardians in his case, came for a friendly visit. This office was modern in the anteroom, but through the glass window on the door of the office, he saw a heavy wood desk with four chairs lined before it. Eric and another boy sat at each end, each held bloody paper towels to their faces. A middle-aged man with a close-cropped brown beard sitting across from them was on the phone—and he didn't look pleased.

After signing in at the counter, Luca was escorted into the office and asked to sit beside his nephew. As soon as he sat, Eric turned his back to him.

Mr. Peterson returned the phone to its cradle and addressed the second boy. "Bryce, are you sure there's no other way to contact your mother?"

When the boy removed the paper towel, Luca saw his bottom lip was split down the center and swollen twice as big as it should be. Lord, don't let his teeth be loose.

"She probably ran out of minutes," Bryce grumbled before wiping the bloody drool from his chin. "Besides that, she worked half the night at the Stop-n-Shop. She usually sleeps until I get home. Later on, she goes to her other job."

"Oh, yeah? Who does she sleep with?" Eric asked. "Or does that change from hour to hour?"

Luca wanted to smack him. They'd have a long talk later.

Bryce tried to climb over Luca to get to Eric, but he pushed him back into his own chair, grabbed the back of Eric's chair and swiveled it around to face the corner. "That was rude, insulting, and uncalled for, young man. If you were a grown man, I'd punch you myself. I will not tolerate anyone talking about a lady that way. Don't you dare say another word unless you're told to."

"How do you know she's a lady?"

Yep, a conversation was in order.

"How can you say she's not? Besides that, I told you to stay quiet."

When Eric turned to pin Luca with a sneer, he saw the bloody nose and swelling next to his left eye. That was going to be colorful by dinnertime. "I bet you haven't heard the things people around here say about

Aunt Joy."

"And you know they're wrong. So, why do you want to put yourself in those idiots' league? Is that what this was about?"

"I never said anything about Miss Sullivan," Bryce shouted.

"Maybe not, but you're a thief." Eric tried to stand, but Luca grabbed his collar in time. "He stole my phone while I was at gym class. He was the only one who went back to the locker room."

"You both walked in here with a three-day suspension for fighting," Mr. Peterson informed the boys. "Your behavior here will make it a week. Eric, if your phone was taken, you should have come here to report it. Bryce, did you take Eric's phone?"

Bryce started shaking his head to deny the accusation when a hip-hop beat sounded from his pocket. It was Eric's ring tone.

Luca held up his own phone to show how he'd caught the culprit. "Damn, Bryce, I was pulling for you, man."

Eric glared at him. "Thanks a lot, Uncle Luca. It's good to know whose side you're on."

Bryce took the phone from his pocket and tossed it in Eric's lap. "You guys don't know what it's like. You've got phones and games and bikes and cool clothes, and you never have to work for anything. Your moms shop all day and go out to eat, while my mom serves them at two different jobs. But she's the one people make fun of. She's the one who never gets anything new." Tears ran down Bryce's cheeks. "I don't want your stupid phone. I just wanted you to see what it's like to not have it."

Mr. Peterson looked sad. It was clear he felt sorry for the boy, but rules had to be enforced. "Will you want to press charges, Mr. Wolff?"

Eric jumped to answer for him. "Yeah!"

Luca put a hand over his mouth. "No."

"Bryce, for stealing and lying, you'll stay after school every afternoon for two weeks—following your suspension. You'll report to the custodian and help him for an hour. I'll take you home and explain all this to your mother."

Bryce dropped his head. "Yes, sir."

On the way home, Eric clung to the car door and didn't say a word. Luca didn't know enough about his nephew to guess what he was thinking. Maybe he did have a lot to learn about the world outside his family.

****

Joy sat beside Luca on a massive sofa in Dr. Johnson's waiting room. She chewed one thumb nail to ragged bits and was now working on the second as they waited for Eric's session to end. The last forty-five minutes seemed like hours.

"You should have called me," she said. "You could have picked me up on your way to the school."

"I was driving my own car," he said, holding up two fingers. "Not enough seats, remember? Besides that, you had a full schedule today. Could you really leave your client halfway finished to run to the school?"

Joy knew he was right, but she hated being left out of matters regarding Eric. "Why didn't you come into the shop when you got back and tell me what was going on?"

Luca rolled his eyes. "I'm not going to air our dirty laundry to all your busybody customers. They're

131

already waiting for Eric to screw up so they can say *I told you so*."

He was right again, dammit. "Do you think he needs to see a doctor? The bruise on his cheekbone is bigger than I've ever seen, and it's close to his eye."

"The school nurse put ice on it right away. It could have been a lot worse. Guys fight—it's the nature of the beast."

Joy let out a gasp when she turned to face him. "Are you saying you think this is okay?"

"Hell, no. Eric was way out of line." Luca crossed his arms and leaned back. "He needs to learn to stand up for himself without fighting."

Joy mimicked his movements and crossed her arms as well. "So, you think this was all Eric's fault."

"I didn't say that. Bryce clearly was in the wrong. But Eric didn't try to resolve the issue with his brain first. That's what he needs to learn."

"I agree," Dr. Johnson said as he followed Eric out of his office.

This was the first time Joy had met Eric's therapist in the flesh. He was an African-American man of medium height and build. She'd guess his age to be in the mid-thirties. He wore an open collar shirt with black jeans and expensive athletic shoes. He shook Luca's hand first, then hers. "Let me give you my card. It has my private number in case you need to contact me after hours." He held the card between two fingers toward her and smiled. "This guy is a little bit of a challenge, but he's coming along."

Joy took the card and tucked it into the pocket on the front of her purse. "I guess you'll be reporting this to Judge Benedict."

"I will, but I'll also report about everything else that's been going on this week. I feel like Eric's making some good progress. I'm not going to let one incident tarnish that." Before he went back to his office, he patted Eric's shoulder. "Think about what I said."

Joy felt as though everyone was making progress with Eric but her. "We'd better get home before Mrs. Washington brings dinner. I bet she's got something great to serve."

"I'm not really hungry," Eric mumbled.

"That's okay." Luca smiled. "More lasagna for me. She always makes lasagna on the last Friday of the month."

Eric stormed to the car, rode home silently, and then went straight to his room.

When Joy thought Mrs. Washington had rung her doorbell, she found Detective Anderson on her stoop instead. She let him in and called for Luca. "It's nice to finally see you again, Detective. Is everything all right?"

"Yes and no," Anderson replied. "I'm not here with bad news this time...or at least not as bad as the first time I came. However, I do have something a little disturbing to discuss with you."

Joy led him toward the kitchen. "Maybe we should sit down at the table, and you can talk while I put on a pot of coffee."

"That would be fabulous."

Luca joined them in the kitchen. "What is this about? I know how busy you detectives are. This isn't a social call."

Joy plugged in the newly prepared percolator and sat with the men. "What could possibly be wrong? No one else has been hurt, I hope."

Anderson took his notebook from his pocket but didn't open it. "That depends on how you look at it. I told Mr. Wolff when I met him that something didn't sit right with me about this case."

Luca sat back with a frown. "I remember. Do you suspect the plane wasn't maintained properly?"

Anderson shook his head. "Your father paid to have a dive team salvage the wreckage. We've been all over every piece they found. We have the records provided by the mechanic. We even have an extra man who witnessed that everything was checked and double checked that morning. Your brother went over the plane again before take-off. It was in pristine condition…except for one thing. The fuel line had been loosened. Both the men who worked in the hanger that morning said it was a brand-new part. They swear they were careful to install it properly, fearing that something like this could happen. They filled the tank hours before the plane left. If there had been a leak, they'd have evidence on the floor. Also, the threads showed wear all the way up, but it had been backed off by a few turns. Like I said before, it was a brand-new part. The packaging was still in the trash barrel. Someone loosened it on purpose."

Was Joy hearing correctly? "Why would anyone want to hurt David and Melissa?"

Luca covered her hand with his. "When you do business to make money, you can often make enemies, as well. I just wouldn't expect David to be a target. He worked internally. He didn't have direct contact with outsiders."

Anderson gave Luca an intense stare. "How about

you, Mr. Wolff. Do you make enemies?"

He grinned and shrugged. "I'm not connected to the family business, but I suppose some people may not like my books."

Anderson flipped open his notebook. "After I found out about the fuel line on your brother's plane, I asked the fire marshal to have an arson team inspect your house in Cocoa Beach."

By now, Joy was even more confused. "I thought you said it was caused by an underground gas leak."

Luca held his palms out. "That's what I was told."

Anderson paused before he replied. "It was hard to track down the cause, but we now know it was intentional. Specialized investigators found evidence of an explosive device under the gas line to your central fireplace. That's the second thing I came to tell you." The detective sat forward and pointed at Luca. "These were both attacks on your family. I don't believe in coincidence. I think this is the same person, and I think this is personal."

They all sat in silence, letting the information soak in for several minutes. The only thing Joy could think about was Eric's safety. Would the judge reconsider his plan if he knew the Wolff family were in danger? She'd be glad when this was over. There was one more issue to address first. "Detective, now that you know the cause of the accident, will you be releasing David and Melissa's remains? We should have the funeral as soon as possible to allow Eric and the rest of the family to move on."

Anderson gave her an odd look. It was a cross between concern and confusion. "What are you talking about? The medical examiner only ordered a few tissue samples to make sure nothing had affected them mentally or physically. Everything came back fine."

He flipped through a few pages of his notebook. "The bodies were released to Daniel Wolff on the tenth of August. He had them both cremated in Tampa before returning to Jacksonville."

Chapter Seventeen

Saturday, September 1—The Confrontation

Luca didn't bother to knock on his father's door at eight the next morning, he still had a key. He also didn't resist Eric who insisted on coming along. After all, the kid was as much a part of the family as he was. The fact that the boy's presence would be an irritation to his father and brother was a bonus. He walked straight to the breakfast room where Daniel sat reading the morning newspaper and poured himself a cup of coffee. "Where's the old man?"

Daniel didn't bother to lower his paper. "In bed with a migraine—he must have sensed you were coming. I'll talk to Father today about having the locks changed." He flipped to the next page. "Your protégé knows he's not welcome here."

Luca found the remark disgusting. "Most grandfathers would enjoy a visit from their only son's child. You haven't even said hello."

Daniel finally set the paper aside and looked at Luca with a sneer. "I don't associate with criminals. You can cut his hair and dress him up, but he's still a crook. You'll find out after you've bailed him out of jail a few times." He turned to Eric. "Why are you here?"

Eric looked him in the eye without wavering. "I want to know where my parents are."

Daniel folded his arms and chuckled. "You don't want to hear my suspicions about that, boy. I don't have to list their sins to you, I'm sure."

Eric's eyes narrowed. "Cut it out, Grand-Dan. You know what I'm talking about."

His grandfather's upper lip curled at the use of the nickname.

"I know you have Mom and Dad's remains. Where are they? Why hasn't there been a funeral?"

Daniel picked up his newspaper again but didn't open it. "I would think that would be obvious. Funerals are unnecessary and costly. Your parents' remains have been placed in the family crypt. I knew a public display would bring in riff-raff, but still, here you are. I hope that Sullivan woman isn't with you. I'd have to have the silver checked." Daniel looked his grandson up and down. "Well, I guess I'd better do that anyway."

"Don't let him get to you, Eric," Luca advised. "He's always cranky before his first bottle and diaper change."

Daniel's face turned so red, it practically radiated heat. "Pretty soon you won't be able to walk around here so freely. After all that's happened, I plan to beef up security. This house is going on lock down. Father has to be protected."

Eric looked at Luca with a crinkled brow. "What's he talking about?"

Luca glared at his brother before turning to Eric with a milder expression. "I intended to talk to you about some information the cops came up with. I didn't want to bother you with it until we had answers about your parent's arrangements."

"The family is under attack," Daniel blurted before Luca could finish. "Luca's house was intentionally blown up, and my plane was sabotaged. I don't suppose you know anything about that."

"My parents were murdered?" Eric asked Luca with a horrified expression. He turned back to Daniel, angry now. "And you think I did it?"

Daniel simply raised both hands, palms toward the ceiling and shoulders high.

Luca had had enough. "Tell the old man we were here."

"Yeah, and tell him he can kiss my ass right beside you," Eric added.

Daniel laughed. "He's beginning to sound a lot like you, Luca."

Eric took a few steps toward his grandfather. "How much would I sound like him if I told you, you can suck my—"

Luca grabbed Eric by the collar of his shirt. "That's enough, Tiger. We're outta here."

****

Joy listened to Eric's account of the visit with tears in her eyes. He finished by saying, "I didn't even get to say goodbye." She knew he was talking about his parents, not Daniel.

The three of them, she, Eric, and Luca, sat around the table while Mrs. Washington heated the pot roast she'd brought by for their dinner. Joy gently placed her hand on Eric's shoulder. "You don't need a funeral to say goodbye, Eric. What made your parents who they were wasn't skin and bone. It was what they had in their hearts."

His eyes widened. "Blood?"

Mrs. Washington popped him on the back with a dish towel. "What are you, a vampire? She's talking about their spirits. The part of them that goes on to heaven...hopefully. In this case, I'm sure of it."

"That's right," Joy affirmed. "I talk to my mom anywhere and anytime I want to. I talk to your mom now, too. I never worry about what was left unsaid or what they're missing. They're with me all the time."

Eric jumped forward. "Do they actually talk back to you, Aunt Joy? I've heard certain people have that power. They have a whole channel about it on cable."

"No." She laughed. "I only talk to the people I love. They don't answer me in words, but sometimes I can feel what they say in my heart."

Eric asked Luca, "Is that true?"

Luca gave Joy a sideways glance. "I never thought about it before, but I guess she's right. I've lost people in the past who still seem to be with me."

Joy knew Luca was talking about the men he'd seen die in combat. They haunted his dreams to this day. She wished she could hug him sometimes...a lot.

"The great thing is," she told Eric, "they're happier after they leave here. They don't feel pain or fear. They're reunited with loved ones who've gone before them. And they watch over people they've left behind. I guess you could call them guardian angels." She glanced Luca's way. "Some of us are blessed with more angels than others."

"Still," Eric declared, "it doesn't seem right to just forget about honoring them with a funeral."

Mrs. Washington sat the roasting pan on the stove top and shut the oven door. "I have a suggestion if everyone doesn't mind me putting in my two cents." When they all turned to her, she continued. "We could put together a really nice memorial service."

Joy was inspired. "That's a great idea. There's a beautiful park near here where your parents used to have picnics and such when they were dating. The weather is so nice this time of year, I could invite Melissa's friends from school and the people she used to work with. They've always asked about her when I've seen them around town."

Mrs. Washington added, "I'll talk to their household staff. They were very loyal. That means Mr. David and Miss Melissa were good bosses. I'm sure they'll want to come, and they can provide a few pictures to put out in a sort of display."

Luca jumped in to offer "Nelson knows the best caterers in town, and Arnold will insist on doing the flowers. Some of David's employees will attend, as long as the old man doesn't find out. Would next Sunday be too soon?"

"Not for us." Mrs. Washington spoke for herself and her two co-workers.

Eric seemed eager. "It's already been a month, I say, the sooner, the better."

Joy hesitated. "Maybe Saturday would be a better idea. Some people like to attend church on Sunday."

Luca looked surprised. "Don't you have clients scheduled that day?"

Joy shook her head. "No, I always take September eighth off." She hadn't meant for them to know that—dammit. "You know, for repairs, maintenance, inventory, that kind of stuff."

"We'll help you with all that afterward," Eric

offered.

Luca gave her a suspicious look. He wasn't buying her excuse.

Joy turned her attention to the stove. "That pot roast smells heavenly."

****

Eric settled into the backyard hammock with his notebook and pen.

Hey, Doc Johnson,

Since I saw you last night a lot has happened—good and bad.

Bad thing—I found out someone purposely killed my mom and dad. If I find out who, I'm going to go medieval on them. Probably the same person blew up my uncle Luca's house. My Grand-Dan says the family is under attack. As far as I'm concerned, they can have him. He's the one I told you is my dad's dad.

Good thing—I got to tell him off. Well, almost. My Uncle Luca dragged me out of there when I really got wound up. But I had good reason to be mad.

Bad thing—I found out Grand-Dan had my parent's bodies cremated and stored in the family tomb. Gross, isn't it? He didn't even tell us.

Good thing—We're planning a memorial service for them. Aunt Joy says they'll be there, and I can say goodbye to them. She says I can talk to them any time, any place. What do you think of that?

Another good thing—they're letting me help. They listen to me just like it's a normal thing. I figure it's because they feel sorry for me being an orphan and all. Still, I like it.

See ya soon,

Eric Wolf is out of the building—haaaaa!!!!

Something on the other side of the window caught Eric's attention. Janet was out there by the sidewalk talking to Mitch Frazier. He was the biggest, meanest guy in ninth grade. It looked like she was giving the meathead a piece of her mind. Maybe he should go out and make sure she's okay.

No, she was storming back inside her house, and meathead was driving off like he was all sad. Good for her.

Chapter Eighteen

Saturday, September 8—A Celebration of Life

Joy couldn't have asked for a more perfect day. The temperature was mild and breezy at seventy-five degrees. The ladies wore the type of dresses you'd see at garden parties, several in pretty hats to shade their faces from the sun. Men stood together in groups after removing their suit jackets and ties.

After several people stood between the eleven-by-thirteen framed photographs of Melissa and David to speak about them, balloons were released against a backdrop of fluffy white clouds. A few butterflies joined in to admire the beautiful bouquets Arnold had set at each table.

The catering staff passed around glasses of lemonade and iced tea. Eric had requested that no alcohol be served. It broke her heart to understand why. His childhood had been marred by alcoholism. She wished for the thousandth time Melissa had come to her with her problems, but that was in the past. It wouldn't do anyone good to look back.

More than a few people remarked on how excellent the food was. Nelson had made the choice of caterer, but Mrs. Washington had supervised every dish. No matter how wonderful it all looked and smelled, Joy couldn't bring herself to eat a bite. It had been almost sixteen years since she'd been to a party this size, and that had been Melissa's wedding. The memory was hard to avoid.

What would Melissa think of the send-off her son had helped plan? They'd all discovered how once Eric put his mind to something he didn't stop at short measures. But perhaps he'd never been as passionate about a project as he had this one. She was eager to feed his enthusiasm in other ways.

This had been important to Eric, and she was glad they could arrange it. She had to admit, though—she wouldn't have known where to start without Luca and Mrs. Washington. Even Nelson and Arnold were willing to work long hours on the project. The fact that Luca's staff hardly knew Melissa and David proved they were motivated by admiration and respect for their employer. If it was important to him, they'd see to it everything went off without a hitch—and it had.

She spotted Luca walking around the outside of the crowd with Eric. Their nephew was already taking on his uncle's traits. Both wore dark dress slacks and starched white shirts open at the collar. Their sleeves were rolled to the elbow with hands in pockets. They never looked down, only straight ahead or facing each other as they spoke. In barely more than three weeks, the street kid they'd picked up at the courthouse was becoming a good man, even if he did still have a few rough edges.

She couldn't stand the thought of losing custody of Eric, but she knew Luca would have to be a big part of his life. That thought didn't bother her as much as it had in the beginning. She and Luca both sincerely wanted what was best for him.

Tricia, Melissa's best friend from high school, waved as she approached. "Joy, I've never been to such a beautiful and uplifting memorial service. Melissa would be so proud of you."

"Thank you, Tricia."

"I always thought Melissa and I would raise our families together and stay best friends until we grew old and gray," the woman continued. "It seemed like she didn't come around much in the last few years, and now she's gone. I just can't wrap my mind around that. I'm heartbroken."

Joy nodded. "I know. She was so young."

She wanted to yell—*Don't you think I miss her? Don't you think I pictured a different outcome for her future? She was my sister.*

Tricia looked around as if checking to see if anyone was listening. "I hope you don't mind, but I have to ask you a personal question."

Joy smiled. "You can ask me anything you like. I can't guarantee I'll answer your question, but you can ask."

That didn't dampen her curiosity. "It's about Eric. I was studying David and Melissa's pictures. They were both so fair. Was Eric adopted?"

"Eric takes after David's mother's family." She didn't know if it was true, but her answer seemed to satisfy Tricia. People could be so rude and intrusive. Who knew that better than she? "You really should give me a call for an appointment, Tricia. I'd be glad to help with those dried out split-ends."

****

Luca put an arm around Eric's shoulders. "The

things you said about your parents were nice. I have to admit I was a little nervous when you walked up in front of everyone."

Eric smiled up at him. "I wouldn't have helped put all this together just to destroy it. But to be honest, I had to reach way back to think of times when we were a happy family. Even now I'm not sure if my parents ever really loved each other. I know you think I'm exaggerating when I say their problems were mainly about me, but I truly believe they only got married because mom was pregnant for me. Don't bother to deny it. I'm pretty good with math."

Stunned by Eric's observation, Luca said, "Your mom made a few mistakes when she was young. We all do. But I can guarantee you; you were not one of those mistakes. She considered you her greatest accomplishment. A lot of families start out that way, you know. Yours isn't the first one that didn't hold up under the test of time. From what I hear, marriage is like taking a stroll through a minefield. You may reach the other side or get blown to high heaven. Your chances are fifty-fifty."

"Do you think you'll ever get married, Uncle Luca?"

"Oh sure. The day hell freezes over."

They both stopped when they saw Mrs. Washington rushing toward them.

The woman was breathing so hard from excitement her chest was heaving. "There's something you should know."

Luca took her by the shoulders. "Slow down and catch your breath. It can't be important enough to have a heart attack over."

"I just got some intel from Doris Graves you'll want to hear, sir."

Eric tilted his head. "Isn't she the bag lady who hangs out at the gas station?"

Mrs. Washington shook her head. "No, that's Deloris. Doris works for the tax office. She said Miss Joy came in yesterday to renew her driver's license."

Luca laughed. "That's not against the law. As a matter of fact, it's pretty much the opposite."

She swatted at Luca. "Oh, I know that. It's what she said after that."

Luca held in his amusement. "Cut to the chase, Mrs. Washington. I'm not getting any younger."

"She said, and I quote—isn't it a shame poor Joy is spending her birthday this way."

"That must be the real reason she was taking the day off." Luca turned to Eric. "Why didn't you tell me it was her birthday?"

Eric scowled. "How was I supposed to know? I didn't have any reason to ask for her ID."

Mrs. Washington rang her hands. "What are we going to do?"

Luca checked the time, four thirty. The guests would be leaving soon, and arrangements were made for clean-up. "I'll take care of it. I'll think of a reason to go into town and get a present, then I'll take her out to a nice restaurant. I know just the place. I'll take my car and head out now. The rest of you can ride with Nelson. Can you watch Eric tonight?"

Eric kicked the dirt. "Cripes, I don't need a babysitter."

Mrs. Washington nodded. "I have a ton of work to do at the new house, but Arnold will be around." She turned to Eric. "Just in case you need anything."

Eric scowled. "Okay, but Uncle Luca, you have to give me two hundred dollars so I can get Aunt Joy a present."

Luca's eyebrows lifted. "Two hundred dollars?"

"I know what I want to give her." Eric smiled. "Trust me, she'll love it."

Chapter Nineteen

Saturday, September 8—A Hot Date

Joy sat on her sofa and removed her shoes. It had been a trying day. She was happy so many people had wonderful memories of her sister to share. She listened to every one of them and smiled, but inside she was deeply depressed.

Over the last few weeks, she'd been busy trying to adjust to Eric, Luca, and their bizarre living situation. Eric's past problems were always on her mind. Would he act out more after the constant monitoring was over?

Then, there was the matter of the PTSD Luca apparently suffered. She'd read his recent book and wondered if pouring the graphic details out on paper was a healthy way to cope. It surprised her to realize how much she cared. No one should have to suffer that way. Not even a Wolff.

It hadn't passed many people's notice that he and Eric were the only Wolffs there today. That was fine with her. It had been a pleasant gathering. Gerald and Daniel Wolff would have made it uncomfortable for the staff and employees. They'd be a curious spectacle to the people of Summer Springs.

She hadn't yet come to terms with the fact that her sister and brother-in-law were intentionally killed before she'd jumped, headlong, into planning today's service. She hadn't really dealt with their deaths at all.

The root cause hadn't hit her until today. She let go of a giant, heart-shaped balloon in purple, Melissa's favorite color. She watched it float higher and higher, knowing it would soon be out of sight—knowing she'd never see it again, just like Melissa.

She still had Eric and prayed she always would. She loved him even more than she'd expected. But all the people connected to her childhood were gone. She hadn't had a great childhood, but her mother had done her best to provide and nurture. Melissa had validated a poor little brown-skinned girl's existence when many others called her a dirty secret, or an unfortunate mistake. Life would never be the same. However, feeling sorry for herself wouldn't help.

Joy looked out the window and saw the sun setting. Another day was over. Perhaps she should just think of today as a beginning rather than an end. But the beginning of what?

Mrs. Washington called from the kitchen doorway, "Miss Joy, Mr. Luca asked me to tell you he has plans for tonight. He'd like you to change into something nice. He'll pick you up in about an hour."

It seemed funny Luca hadn't mentioned this earlier. "Did he say what kind of plans?"

The older woman shook her head with a smile. "He only said that you both needed to get out of the house and take a break."

Joy looked down at what she was wearing. "I don't have anything nicer than this black dress."

Mrs. Washington pointed behind herself. "The blue skirt and white top hanging in the laundry room is very attractive. I think he just wants you to be comfortable."

The other outfit would be cooler, but would it be too casual? She remembered her humiliation when Barbara had made fun of her at the courthouse. Her mother had been more style conscious. She'd look for something in her things. Joy rarely left the house. Everything she was used to seemed to be getting turned upside-down. Then she had another thought. "What about Eric?"

"Arnold will stay until you get back. Don't worry. They'll probably order a pizza and watch a horror movie." The older woman shuddered dramatically. "Just go and enjoy yourself."

"Where is Luca?" Joy asked. "He didn't come back with us and his car isn't in the parking lot."

"No telling what that man is up to." Mrs. Washington walked back to the kitchen with a sly smile.

What was going on?

****

Luca tapped on the bathroom door. It wasn't Joy's habit to spend a lot of time dressing. When she came out, it was worth the wait. She looked stunning in a full-skirted, orange sundress and white sandals. Her hair had been pulled back into a puffy ponytail with a white bow. How had such a tiny touch of make-up turned her eyes greener? "Are you ready?"

Joy ran her hands down the front of the skirt. "I'm sorry it took so long. This dress had been in a trunk. I had to iron it."

He had to force himself to stop staring. "Don't be sorry. You look…amazing." He hadn't gone out in a while, but this wasn't his first date. Was this a date? "I hope you're hungry. I know the owner of the best Italian restaurant in the city."

"That sounds good."

Joy seemed a little awkward and shy. How would she take the next part of the evening? "First, I have a surprise for you. My sources tell me today is your birthday. I can hardly let a thing like your thirtieth birthday go by without a celebration." He took her hand and led her out the front door.

"Oh, no, you really shouldn't. I don't give a lot of thought to my birthday. It's just another..."

Next to Luca's car in the parking spot closest to her front door was a small, green convertible. It had a huge white bow on the hood. Mrs. Washington, Nelson, Arnold, and Eric stood on the opposite side. They all shouted, "Happy Birthday!" Tears came to her eyes. They were starting to think of her as part of the family.

"Oh my God! It's a car!" Joy ran around at twice before stopping with an expression of misery. "I can't afford a car. The payments on this thing must be astronomical."

Luca couldn't believe she'd think such a thing of him. "I wouldn't buy you something you had to pay for. It's paid in full, tagged and insured. The keys are in the ignition, and the bill of sale is in the glove box. It would only be polite for you to drive tonight. If you want to celebrate more, I'll drive back."

Luca directed her to Maria's Little Italy. It wasn't the fanciest restaurant in town, but it was his favorite. As they pulled into the parking lot, they could hear an Italian song crooning from the speakers on the patio.

Joy clapped her hands. "Oh! Look at the umbrella tables. Can we sit outside? The weather is perfect."

She looked so excited, Luca couldn't refuse. "First we have to go inside and say hello. Momma would never forgive me otherwise." He walked around the rear of the car to open her door and gave her a hand to guide her inside.

Joy laughed. "You call the manager Momma?"

"She's the owner and cooks as well, and I certainly had better call her Momma. She claims she was in labor for me for two days. I think that's an exaggeration."

"I hope so." Joy laughed.

As soon as they'd stepped inside his attractive, dark-haired mother rushed toward them. "My bambino! I'm so glad to see you. I heard about David and his pretty little wife. It's so tragic." She kissed him on both cheeks then looked curiously at Joy. "I'm glad you aren't alone this time. Who is this beautiful companion of yours?"

Joy saw a blush on Luca's cheeks when he turned to her. "Momma, I'd like you to meet Joy. We're here to celebrate her birthday."

His mother took Joy's hands and kissed both of her cheeks. "My son spends much too much time by himself. I'm glad you're here. I just took a pan of lasagna from the oven. You should eat and drink and dance. My son is an excellent dancer. I made him take lessons. His father was so mad."

Joy laughed. "I bet he was."

Luca hardly had time to talk to Joy. He knew every employee, and each one stopped by the table to tell her a funny story about him as a child. She didn't seem to mind. As a matter of fact, she laughed the whole time. After she'd eaten half her lasagna and a few bites of tiramisu, he stood and gave her his hand. "Could I have the honor of a dance, birthday girl?"

Joy looked nervous. "I've had two glasses of wine. I don't usually drink. You may have to hold me up."

"It would be my pleasure."

She was able to stand on her own and danced quite well. Luca loved the way she felt in his arms. Thank heaven for slow music. "I feel fortunate to share your birthday, considering the competition."

"What competition?" Joy asked. "I haven't been on a date in ages."

He quirked a brow. "I think it's pretty obvious Dr. Johnson has his eye on you."

Joy laughed. "You're being ridiculous. Why would a successful man like him want anything to do with me?"

Luca eyed her severely. "I like to consider myself fairly successful, and I find you incredibly attractive."

She slapped his shoulder. "Stop it. You're playing with me because I'm a little tipsy."

He spun her at a climax in the song. "No, I'm not. I think you're stunning. It irritates the hell out of me that Dr. Johnson thinks so, too. I just may be a little jealous. *Let me give you my card. It has my private number in case you need to contact me after hours.* Do you remember him saying that? He didn't give the card to me."

Joy looked surprised. "He gave me his business card, so you gave me a convertible. Is that what I'm hearing?"

"All's fair in love and war—that's all I'm saying." Had he also had a little too much wine? When she tipped her head back and closed her eyes, she didn't realize her lips were mere inches from his. "You have the most beautiful lips. I've always wondered what they'd feel like." He gently touched her lower lip. "And now I'd love to find out how they taste."

She opened her eyes with a worried brow. "Aren't you afraid your mother will see? She may not like you being so close to…someone like me."

"Ridiculous. My mother loves you." He kissed her lips, so soft, so lush. He couldn't stop. Her breath was sweeter than the wine they'd drank. He held her tighter. Her body was small but seemed to fit him perfectly.

The music stopped, and she pulled away. "We should go home."

He wished he could read more into that sentence, but he knew the evening had come to an end. He said goodbye to his mother and led Joy to the passenger seat of her new car. A few minutes later, he heard her sigh contentedly and looked over to see she was sleeping. Two glasses of wine were all she could hold. Would she remember their kiss? He was sure he wouldn't forget it for a long time…if ever.

She still slept as he made his way through Summer Springs to her street. That's when he saw the thick, black smoke covering the clouds above her house.

Chapter Twenty

Sunday, September 9—Up in Flames

Luca patted Joy's knee. "Wake up, Joy. Honey, you have to get up."

Her entire body felt too heavy to move. Even her eyelids seemed to be weighted down. She just wanted to sleep. "What time is it?"

"Twelve-thirty. We have to get out of the car."

Her nose wrinkled. "Are we home? It smells bad here. I swear it's not my fault."

Luca's voice sounded strained. "It's smoke, baby. The house is on fire."

"What?"

Joy cracked her eyes open a tiny bit. All she made out were flashing red lights. They weren't in her parking area. This was Mrs. Rogers' house, next door. Why were people shouting? She forced herself to sit up straighter. The chaos around her home made her heart pound. Smoke caused everything to appear dreamlike, but it wasn't a dream. Luca's last words finally registered in her mind. The house is on fire. Her house.

A man in a yellow vest appeared at Luca's window. "You people will have to move along."

"This is our house—or her house." Luca fumbled for words. "We live here."

The man pointed over his shoulder. "You'll need to speak to the chief. He's behind the ladder truck." He moved on to a group of people standing on the sidewalk.

As she stepped out of the car, she felt a little dizzy. The two glasses of wine were history, but adrenaline pumped through her veins. This was no time for drama. She had to pull herself together. Her home and livelihood were at stake.

She glanced across the street and saw a police car. Arnold looked at her from the back window. "What's going on?" she asked an officer as she pointed at the car.

The policeman looked at the car. "We found him behind the house when we arrived. He says he works for you."

Luca dropped her hand. She hadn't realized he'd been holding it. "I'll take care of this."

The policeman continued, "He also said he was looking for your nephew."

A horrible image came into her mind. "Eric? Isn't Eric here? Is he inside?" She began to run toward the house. "Eric!"

A firefighter grabbed her arm. "There's no one inside, ma'am. Please don't put yourself in danger."

Luca pointed at Arnold. "I have to talk to the man in the car. He was supposed to be here with my nephew. I need to find out where Eric is."

When the officer opened his rear car door, they could see Arnold's hands were cuffed behind his back. His left arm still wasn't one-hundred-percent. She knew he must be in pain.

"Sir, I don't know where Eric is." Arnold was in a

panic. "One minute he was in the kitchen, talking on his phone, and then I must have fallen asleep. The next thing I knew, he was gone. I rode around looking for him for a while. When I decided to come back and see if he'd returned, the salon was on fire. I called emergency, but then the cops didn't believe I belonged here."

Joy was surprised when Detective Anderson walked toward them. "Mr. Wolff, isn't this the man you said was at your house the day of the explosion?"

Luca had his phone to his ear, but he held his hand over it to reply. "He didn't do this."

"Why are you here?" Joy asked Anderson. "You're from the Jacksonville Police Department. The Duval County Sheriff's office usually handles things here in Summer Springs."

"I have a flag on your name and the Wolffs in the central database. If any reports are made on you, your cars, or addresses, I'm notified. Something like this could be connected to my case."

The firefighter in Chief's gear approached. "You're fortunate, ma'am. The only apparent damage was to the hair salon."

"Yeah, lucky." Joy barely forced the words from her throat.

"Aunt Joy!" At the edge of the lawn, another police officer was placing handcuffs on Eric.

She yelled at Anderson, "Why are they arresting my nephew?"

The detective's expression was gloomy. "I'm sorry, Miss Sullivan, but he'd left the house without permission shortly before the fire was discovered—and with his criminal record—"

Luca was enraged. "This is ridiculous. I swear there'll be hell to pay if that boy is hurt. My lawyer will meet you at the station."

Anderson nodded. "I'd like you both to come to the station as well. It's too much to believe that all this is a coincidence."

Joy started to walk up the lawn. "I need to get a few things from the house."

The fire chief stood in her way. "I'm sorry, ma'am, I can't let anyone inside until I'm sure it's safe."

Eric yelled to her as they opened the back door of another patrol car to put him inside. "Aunt Joy, get the box! Look in the box! It's for you!"

She looked back to see a shoebox on the ground where he'd first appeared. It had a pink bow on the top. A cop removed the vented lid and lifted out a round grayish-tan and black handful of fur.

****

Eric had been in the back of patrol cars before, but he was never as angry as he was tonight. He'd cleaned up his look and had put real effort into changing his attitude. The scuffle with Bryce had taken place in the heat of the moment. He'd fallen back into an old habit. Just one little set-back. But it seemed he wasn't the only one who had a hard time getting over the past.

"Remember me, kid?" This came from the cop in the front passenger seat. "I had to run your ass down after you boosted a six-pack from the store on Eleventh Avenue. I wouldn't have recognized you if they hadn't given me your name. It's pretty smart of you to change your description. You have any warrants against you? We'll find out at the station, you know. Remember kid, no matter what you do to your hair, your fingerprints don't change."

"I didn't do anything. I was just going home after I picked up a present for my aunt."

The cop behind the wheel laughed. "Yeah, sure. What store stays open after midnight?"

"And I know where you live," the other cop reminded him. "Summer Springs is a long way from your neighborhood."

"I live in Summer Springs now. I live with my aunt and uncle."

The first cop laughed. "The parents finally got tired of bailing your sorry ass out of jail?"

Eric was suddenly glad they'd secured his hands. At that moment, it was good for their safety. "No, you jelly-filled asshat, they died. Don't you watch the news? My parents were David and Melissa Wolff."

It didn't matter what he wore or how his hair was cut, the cops had only taken a single glance at him and pulled out the cuffs. The tears in Aunt Joy's eyes had ripped his heart out. Uncle Luca looked like he was ready to chew up nails and spit out tacks.

Luca had been a warrior, and his aunt had grown up poor, but neither of them was used to seeing this side of his life. It was a way of life he'd chosen as a stupid kid and already regretted. Eric had acted out to embarrass and punish his parents and look how that turned out. They were both dead without a pleasant word between any of them for years, and he was on his way back to juvie.

Would his aunt and uncle decide he wasn't worth the trouble? Where would he go from here? If he stayed locked up through his birthday, he'd be moved to level three. He didn't know if he'd survive a week there.

They might put him in a group home where his chances were just as slim. If either of his grandfathers had anything to do with it, he'd be on the next flight to Samoa for boot camp school. They thought his dad had agreed with that plan, but he'd only said he did to get them off his back.

He wondered what Doc Johnson would have to say about all this. Would he think he'd set the fire, too? He'd have to tell him about it when the doc asked why he hadn't written in his journal tonight.

Uncle Luca had a new house waiting for him, but what would Aunt Joy do? Everything she'd worked for was probably gone. Was that his fault? Probably. Most everything was.

They pulled into the parking lot. On the ramp to the back of the city building was his uncle Luca looking angry and disheveled, Mr. Meyers all rumpled and sleepy, and the slick lawyer who'd sat beside Luca in the courtroom. He looked like a plastic doll in a sharply pressed suit. Eric didn't know the guy, but he did know he didn't like him.

The cop he'd been familiar with was the one to take him from the back of the patrol car. "Listen, kid, I'm sorry about your parents. I can see how something like that could cause a guy to rethink his life. If you really want to change your ways—good for you. I hope it works out for you."

"Thanks," Eric mumbled.

The cop added, "And if you go so straight you decide to become a cop, give me a call. I'd help you out."

"I appreciate the offer, but I doubt I'll go that way. I've kind of been thinking I'd like to join the marines after I graduate."

"You want to be a jarhead?" The cop let out a short burst of laughter. "Hope it works out for you. I mean that."

Chapter Twenty-One

Sunday, September 9—Get Out of Jail

Luca paced inside a small room where he and Michael Knight waited for Eric. "I feel like I'm losing grip of this situation. I can't seem to do anything but rub Joy the wrong way. She's probably looking forward to the end of this sixty-day trial period."

Knight puffed out a short laugh. "Aren't you? That tiny house and the village it's set in would be driving me crazy by now."

Luca thought about it for only a moment. "It's actually pretty nice. I get a lot of time to work, the house is comfortable, and the people are friendly. I take a run through the park when I get stuck on a scene. There's no place like it in the city. My staff loves Joy. She's a great housekeeper and an excellent cook. I've probably gained a few pounds. She does all she can to please everyone."

Knight wiggled his brows. "I wouldn't mind her giving me a little pleasure—if you know what I mean. She wouldn't even have to cook for me."

A hot wash of rage poured down Luca's body. It would be a cold day in hell before this jerk would touch a hair on Joy's head. Just the fact that he'd thought about her that way made Luca want to punch his lights out. But he needed Knight to help straighten out this mess, so he bit his tongue.

Knight continued, "She hasn't found out about anything she can use against you, has she?"

Luca put his hands in his pockets and leaned against the back wall. "I don't know…maybe."

"What do you mean? What happened?"

Luca spoke in a lower tone. "Well, there was one night when I had an episode with my PTSD while I was sleeping. Living in such close quarters, you don't have a lot of privacy when something like that happens."

Knight frowned as he sat on the table top. "Damn man, I didn't know. That could be considered a mental disorder. I don't think it would affect the way you raise Eric, but she could use it to her advantage."

Luca went further with his admission. "After it happened, I kind of made an inappropriate remark. You have to understand, I was a little out of it."

"Not good, but don't worry. I have an ace up my sleeve. I could ruin her if it starts looking bad for you. I don't leave things like this to chance. I don't like to lose."

He'd suspected from the beginning this man was unscrupulous. But for now, Eric and Arnold needed his full attention. "I don't want to think about that right now. I just want to get this FUBAR straightened out."

"FUBAR?"

"Yeah, that's a military thing. It means effed-up-beyond-recognition, reason, or repair."

"Don't worry," Knight reassured him. "I'm on the job. If they want a lamb to send to the slaughter, I'll make sure it's Arnold, not the kid."

Luca narrowed his eyes and pointed at Knight.

"For the fees you're charging me, you'd better make sure it's neither of them. I can promise you, they didn't do this."

****

The sergeant at the front desk placed a hand on each side of the shoe box and looked inside. "Does it bite?"

Joy jerked the box from his hands. "No, but I do, and you don't want to test me tonight."

"Do you realize that you just threatened an officer of the law, ma'am?"

"I'll be doing a lot worse if I don't get to put my nephew in his own bed tonight. Where is he? I don't want anyone asking him a single question unless I'm with him."

The sergeant turned to his computer. "Who's your nephew?"

Joy spoke very precisely. "Eric Wolff, W-O-L-double F."

"Oh," he groaned, "I know him well. What has he done this time?"

Joy released a growl of frustration. "He hasn't done anything. I want to know where he is this minute."

The sergeant pointed to his computer screen. "He's in an interrogation room with his guardian and lawyer. I'm afraid they're the only people we can let inside."

Joy crossed her arms and leaned toward him. "I'm also his guardian. I want to see him. I should be in there, too."

"Have you ever seen one of our interrogation rooms, ma'am? The closet in my studio apartment is bigger. We can't let anyone else inside. Four people is the maximum capacity."

"He didn't do anything. He's a good kid. Arnold, the other man they brought in, didn't do anything, either. You people are wasting time. You should be out looking for bad guys."

The sergeant tapped on his keyboard a few times. "Arnold...here he is. They aren't under arrest, ma'am. They were simply brought in for questioning."

Joy shook her finger at him. "They were both cuffed and put in the back of squad cars like common criminals...right in front of our neighbors. My business is at that location. What do you suppose my customers are going to say?" She ran a finger down the puppy's back when he began to whine. "Can I have a glass of water?"

When the desk sergeant handed Joy a paper cup filled with water she drank half, then carefully tore the top part of the container off and sat the remaining water inside the box.

The sergeant watched as the puppy lapped up most the water. "You realize it'll probably have to *go* after it drinks that."

"I'll be sure to bring him back to you when he does."

The puppy stumbled around the box with a full belly. The man reached in and patted his head with one finger. "What's his name?"

In all the commotion, she hadn't had time to think about it. "I don't know yet."

He lifted the dog's face to look at him. "What is he?"

Joy turned her nose up to show she still wasn't happy. "He's a miniature pug. I've always wanted one."

"A mini-pug? That's cute."

"Yes, he is."

"I guess you could say he's a mug!"

Joy finally smiled. "Excellent! That's his name—Mugsy. I'm going to teach him to bite people I don't like, so watch yourself."

The sergeant whistled to see if Mugsy would look up—he did.

Joy looked the sergeant up and down. "Why do you live in a studio apartment? It doesn't seem right for a grown man."

"I'm a grown man with two ex-wives and three kids. Any more questions?"

She thought about asking why he'd made the same mistake twice, but then Detective Anderson walked in.

"Can we sit?" Anderson asked as he led her to a row of padded folding chairs by the wall. He looked like he hadn't slept in days. "I'm afraid the fire marshal found signs of arson in your shop."

Joy's eyes widened. "Are you sure? Maybe it was a short in one of the wires."

The detective shook his head. "Definitely not. Someone broke into the door through the glass. They wadded up a bunch of towels and thin cotton material and put them in all the chairs. Then, they opened up boxes full of chemicals you had stored and poured them out. They threw in a few matches and lit the place up. Luckily, I don't think the chemicals burned the way they'd expected. The fire didn't spread past the shop. The house will still have to pass an inspection to see if it's safe. Wiring inside the walls could have been affected, maybe the pipes as well. You won't be able to go back inside until that's taken care of. Then you'll need to air the place out, clean, and try to get the smoke smell out of everything. I have to warn you, it'll be a mess."

Goosebumps stood on Joy's arms. "So you're telling me I've lost my business, and I have no place to stay. I have to find a job with only the clothes on my back. Why would someone do this to me?"

Anderson patted her hand. "I'm not sure you were the target. Mr. Wolff's house was blown up before your sister's death. Someone purposely killed her and her husband. From what I hear, the three of them were close at one time. I suspect the same person may be after him."

Joy shook her head. "What have I gotten myself into? What have we gotten Eric gotten into?"

"Don't forget, Eric is also a Wolff. If this is some kind of attack against the family, he could be in danger, too."

Chapter Twenty-Two

September 9—Alibis and Getaways

The questioning was finally over. As the four of them headed to Joy's car, she told them what Detective Anderson said.

Luca sat in the driver's seat. "I can see how that could happen. No one knows you have a car yet. They probably saw my car was the only one in the lot and assumed I was home."

Eric held onto the headrest from the back to move closer to the conversation. "But any of us could have been with you."

Luca nodded and turned the key to start the engine. "That's true. Fortunately, no one was home. I guess we should go back there so I can move my car out of the way. Arnold, I hope you'll want to start on repairs right away."

Arnold sat against the back seat, arms folded and eyes closed. "All over it, sir."

Luca yawned. "Mrs. Washington says the house is ready and there's a bed for everyone. I don't know about you people, but I could use some sleep."

Joy turned in her front passenger seat and looked at each of the others. "Why wasn't anyone home? Where were you, Eric?"

"I'm sorry I went AWOL like that again," he replied. "I found out where to pick up the pup and didn't want to wake Arnold up. It wasn't far."

Arnold opened his eyes. "I fell asleep watching television. I'm sorry."

Joy leveled a hard stare at Eric. "So, you were running the streets all by yourself!"

"It gets better," Luca interrupted. "During the interview Eric told us he was with Bryce. He's the one who turned him on to the dog. The two of them hung out until minutes before Bryce's mom got home from her night job. The cops had to corroborate Eric's alibi, so now Bryce is going to be in hot water at home, as well."

Joy asked, "Isn't that the boy Eric fought with at school?"

"Yep," Luca confirmed. "Now it seems they're best friends."

Luca saw the confusion on her face. Women didn't understand how these things worked. When a man found something to respect about an enemy, they could overlook the past. It was human nature. Women, however, never forgot anything.

The smell of smoke was still detectable when they pulled into the four-car lot near the burned shop…the empty four-car lot.

Luca's heart nearly leaped out of his chest. "Where the hell is my car!"

While Arnold called Nelson to find out if he'd moved the car, Luca called the police to see if it had been removed by them or the fire department. Both came away with negative answers. The classic sports car had been stolen.

Joy pointed to the left side of the lot. "I'm sure I saw it right there by the fence last night."

Luca slapped the steering wheel. "We had a house fire and a car stolen in one night? What the hell? Did some voodoo priestess get pissed and put a curse on me?"

Eric narrowed his eyes in speculation. "Maybe it was the same person who sat the fire. He could have been watching from the crowd of neighbors and saw us leave with the cops."

"It's a possibility," Luca agreed. "I'll drop you guys at the house and go back to the station to fill out a report with the police."

"You know they're going to think I took it," Eric remarked. "We can't prove when it was taken, and they blame me for everything."

Luca supposed he was right. A bad reputation was hard to live down.

****

Arnold and Nelson both wanted to go with Luca to the police station to watch after his safety. Instead, they were ordered to stay at home and look after Joy and Eric. She didn't see the need in it. She didn't have any enemies. Also, the house was in a gated community, had an iron fence all around, and a state-of-the-art security system.

Luca's house was enormous with six bedrooms, six bathrooms, and a huge room just for playing games. This was where Eric would live if his uncle won guardianship. The boy seemed to take all the amenities for granted. He was used to this lifestyle. What must her tiny house look like to them? She didn't even have a way to pay the bills now.

The bedroom Mrs. Washington led her to was incredible. Besides a huge bed and dresser, it had a little settee and stationary desk. The wood furniture looked like it had all been finished in warm honey. The walls were painted pale blue. The soft features were a combination of patterns in white and yellow with hints of the same blue here and there.

"You have remarkable skills in decorating, Mrs. Washington. This room couldn't be lovelier."

The older woman smiled with pleasure. "I can't take all the credit. Mr. Wolff picks out the furniture and colors, I just take it from there."

There was another talent of the amazing Luca Wolff.

She opened a door at the back of the room to find a private bath. The fixtures were white with brushed silver. It had a glass-enclosed shower in the corner, but she was more fascinated by the claw-footed tub. The walls were the same pale blue as the bedroom. Thick yellow towels trimmed in lace hung on the racks. What kind of price tag had those come with? If she had a stitch of clean clothes to change into, she'd take full advantage of this room. Joy caught a glimpse of herself in the mirror. Her makeup was smudged, and her hair stood out like she'd been out in a hurricane. When Mrs. Washington left to answer a ringing phone, she washed her face and fingered her hair into a loose braid.

Back in the bedroom, she opened another door. It hid a vast walk-in closet. Seeing the bare rods and shelves drove home how dire her situation really was. There was so much to worry over, but right now she was exhausted.

She found a basket in the corner and lined it with

one of the towels. No more shoebox for her little Mugsy. Next, she called Barbara Allgood. The first order of business would be informing the court of their move. Michael Knight was probably taking care of it, but she wanted to show that she was just as responsible.

After they'd talked about the fire and their move to Luca's house, Barbara asked, "So, what's it like?"

"What's it like to be homeless, or losing my only means of income?"

"Neither. I want to know what the magnificent Luca Wolff lives like. Tell me about his house."

"Have you ever seen the movie *The Great Gatsby*? It's kind of like that, but better and more modern."

"Do you think he's into older women? Oh, never mind. I don't want to set myself up for disappointment. Just enjoy your vacation while you can."

"Vacation! I have to find a job. My insurance isn't going to cover all this when it does finally come through—which will take forever."

"What about the money your sister left you? Knight made it sound like a fortune."

"I haven't heard anything about it."

"I'll give him a call and find out what's holding it up."

Just as she was about to lie down on the king-sized bed for a nap, Mrs. Washington called through an intercom on the nightstand and asked her to come downstairs to the sitting room. What now? She could barely keep her eyes open.

Two ladies in the parlor fussed over a couple racks of gorgeous women's clothes. Their pink smocks had the logo of an exclusive boutique in Jacksonville she'd never had the nerve to walk into.

Mrs. Washington looked up when she came through the door. "Mr. Wolff said to see that you have enough clothes to last at least a week."

"I can't afford this," Joy cried.

Mrs. Washington waved away her concerns. "Don't worry about the bill. He insists on taking care of it."

Joy was tired. She wasn't able to hold back tears and racking sobs. She ran back up the stairs to the guest room. She'd become a charity case. This was an all-new low.

Chapter Twenty-Three

Monday, September 10—Further Complications

"Slow down, you little monster. If you keep eating like that you're going to explode."

Joy cracked open one eye and found Eric, sitting on the floor beside the dresser watching Mugsy eat from a matched pair of silver bowls. A fluffy blue dog bed sat nearby.

She groaned and rubbed her eyes. "Oh my God, I'm a horrible dog mom. How am I going to take care of a growing boy?"

"It shouldn't be too hard," Eric assured her. "I'm fairly self-sufficient."

Joy sat upright in her bed and looked around the spacious bedroom. "I imagine you'd prefer to live in a house like this. My place must seem like a shack compared to what you're used to."

"Can I be honest?" he asked.

Joy felt a lump form in her throat. "Of course."

"I like both places. I don't want to give up either one. There's a lot of fun stuff to do here. Especially when Uncle Luca has time to show me how to shoot hoops and lift weights and stuff. He has all the movie channels and a home theater to watch them. I could have a hell of a party here."

He sat Mugsy in his new bed and rose to sit beside Joy. "On the other hand, my friends are in Summer Springs. Believe it or not, I even like the school. Janet speaks to me every time I see her in the hall or on the bus. I'm building up the nerve to ask her out pretty soon. Sure, people there know I have money, but it's not a big deal…you know? Since me and Bryce called a truce, I've met a lot of his friends. They're cool. I've gotten kind of used to helping you out around the house too. It kind of makes me feel like the man of the house. And let's face it, you're a better cook than anybody else in the world. I'm not just talking cookies, either."

Luca appeared in the doorway. "I'd have to say your meatloaf is one of the best things I've ever tasted. You are aware that Mrs. Washington is a seasoned veteran, so I'm risking my life by saying that, but it's the truth."

Joy pushed her hair out of her face. "Are you mad at me about the clothes? I must have looked like a lunatic, storming out on those nice girls. You have to understand, I'm not used to being a charity case. Between the car, my birthday, the fire, the police, no sleep…this has all hit me pretty hard."

"The clothes are not charity, they're a gift."

That's when Joy spotted a pile of pink boxes by the door. "You didn't!"

"I did—a week's worth. I can't have you wandering around in the same clothes every day. I don't know when we'll be allowed back in your house."

She wrinkled her nose. "Mrs. Washington picked them out?"

"No!" Luca laughed. "I'd trust the woman with my life, but do I look that crazy? I picked them out myself.

177

I have a good eye for a person's individual style."

She shook her head. "It's too much money."

Luca sat on the side of her bed and patted Mugsy's head. "Have you ever heard the old saying, money doesn't buy happiness? That's bullshit. Helping others out when they're in need makes me very happy. You'll have money soon, and you'll see what I mean—which leads me to one of the reasons I came in to talk to you. I sponsor a women's shelter in the city. The women there are often in pretty bad shape when they arrive, but they have to go out and find jobs to help them get back on their feet. I wondered if you'd have time to help them with their hair and nails, maybe a little makeup, too. I'd be willing to pay whatever you charge."

"What a wonderful idea. I'd be happy to do it. All I'd need are a few supplies."

He dusted his hands together. "Great, that's settled. Now for the next order of business."

Eric groaned from the corner. "I hope it's food."

"I'm hungry, too." Joy admitted. "I didn't have breakfast or lunch. Maybe I should help Mrs. Washington put dinner on the table."

Luca laughed. "It's a little late for that. She's serving breakfast in fifteen minutes. Just enough time for you to get a shower and change into some fresh clothes."

"Breakfast! How long have I been sleeping? What day is it?"

"It's Monday morning," Eric informed her.

When Luca got up to leave, Joy stopped him. "You said there was something else you wanted to discuss."

Luca stopped in the doorway. "Michael Knight is coming by this evening. He's asked your attorney to be here as well. He said there's been a development in our case, and it involves both of us."

Eric cleared his throat. "Don't you mean the three of us? I intend on being part of this show from now on. I'm not a little kid."

Luca nodded. "You're right. We'll all meet at seven tonight. Why don't you get a head start on those waffles, Eric? Your aunt and I will be down in a minute."

As soon as Eric left the room, Luca sat back down on the edge of the bed beside her. He played with the end of her braid. "You were a little tipsy last night. Do you remember our kiss?"

"I remember, but I don't intend to repeat it."

His expression was pure disappointment. "No?"

She scrambled out of bed on the opposite side. "Not until I have a shower, put on fresh clothes, and find a toothbrush."

"Well, I guess I can wait a little longer."

He left the room smiling.

****

Luca stayed at his writing desk until dinner was served at six o'clock. He was pleased to see that Joy and Mrs. Washington were working together on the meal. His housekeeper hadn't found many women she could make friends with and none she'd allow in her kitchen. He was especially pleased that Joy took the lead on making the meatloaf.

Along with the fantastic food, Luca was delighted that Joy had chosen an outfit he'd picked as a favorite. It was a casual, gauzy dress in a colorful print. He'd noticed she liked to go barefoot after working all day. She was comfortable enough at his house to do the same. He found it incredibly adorable and sexy.

Eric dominated the conversation planning his birthday party. Luca didn't know what the hurry was, but he didn't have any objections to his nephew's suggestions. The idea was to turn the game room into an arcade. It was practically that already. All teenagers seemed to need was a way to burn off the hundreds of calories they consumed at an hourly rate. At that very moment, Eric was quickly polishing off a bowl of rocky road ice cream he and Joy had both passed on.

"Sir," Nelson called as formally as ever, "Miss Allgood and Mr. Knight have both arrived. They're waiting in the sitting room."

"Thank you, Nelson. We'll be right there. Could you ask Mrs. Washington to bring coffee?"

Nelson bowed. "Certainly, sir."

He saw Joy's complexion had paled, but Eric pursed his lips and narrowed his eyes defiantly. "I want everyone to relax. Whatever this is about is probably minor. Remember, we are a united front. No matter how this situation turns out, we work together. We still have five weeks to prove that."

Barbara Allgood made her preference known right away. She kissed Joy's cheek in greeting, and then turned to Eric. "My goodness, you look like you've grown a few inches already. It must be your Aunt Joy's delicious cooking. And your hairstyle is fabulous. Obviously, she knows what young people your age like these days. I was afraid you'd end up with a military crew cut and a diet of K-rations."

Mrs. Washington cleared her throat from the doorway. She looked ready to serve the tray of hot coffee over the other woman's head. "They're called

MREs these days, Miss Allgood, meals-ready-to-eat." She placed the tray on the sideboard and added as she left, "We've come a long way since World War Two."

Luca stifled a laugh and announced, "Please help yourself to the coffee. I'd like to get started with this meeting. It's been a long day.

Michael Knight sat in the biggest chair in the room and addressed Eric first. "I'm sure you'd find this all pretty boring. Don't you have some homework or a video game to get to?"

Eric looked in Luca's direction. When his uncle raised his chin to him, he knew he was expected to answer for himself. "Both of my guardians have agreed to let me stay. It's my future under discussion, and I'm old enough to provide input and opinions."

Barbara straightened from the coffee tray. "I was under the impression this meeting was about Joy's inheritance."

"Actually, it's about the whole ball of wax," Knight informed her. "I wanted to speak to you all face to face, even though I won't be representing Luca Wolff any longer. I'm dropping this case immediately."

"I can't say I'll miss you," Luca sneered. "But I'd appreciate an explanation."

Knight gave the room a big smarmy smile. "Here it is in a nutshell. Both of your inheritances and Eric's guardianship are being challenged by a third party. Since I've been employed by that party for many years, I think it best to represent him in this matter. The proper paperwork has been filed with the court, and you'll receive word shortly."

Luca jumped from his seat. "You can't mean my father. He may be a worm, but he's man enough to face me in a fight."

Knight waved his hand as though he was calming a child. "There's no need to get riled. Your father isn't even aware of this yet. No, I happen to work for Eric's actual next-of-kin."

Luca's face visibly paled. "Daniel?"

"No way," Eric jumped in. "Grand-Dan hates me. Why would he do this?"

Knight calmly sat his coffee on the side table. "All I can say is, he will do it. He's going to fight to see that all your parents' money is awarded to you and he'll be in control of it. He's doing this for you, Eric."

Luca's voice was louder than he'd intended. "To hell with the money. He's never done anything for the boy before. Why now?"

Knight crossed one leg over the other and steepled his fingers. "It would truly be best for you and Miss Sullivan to back off and let this happen. I have information neither of you would want to have exposed to the media."

Barbara finally found her voice. "What kind of information?"

"I'll do both parties the courtesy of keeping that to myself unless it has to be used in court. I do have some ethics, you know."

"No, I don't know," Luca remarked. "I could see when we met you were a snake. I should have listened to my instincts. If you don't leave my house immediately, I can't guarantee your safety."

"Is that a threat?" A sound from the door caused Knight to turn in that direction.

Arnold stood with his arms folded over his chest scowling. Mrs. Washington and Nelson had his back.

Arnold spoke for the three of them. "You have two minutes to get inside your car."

"This is outrageous." Knight looked down when he felt his ankle warming. Mugsy was sticking by his new family. He had his leg raised and was in the process of relieving his tiny bladder on the man's sock and very expensive ostrich-skin loafer.

Chapter Twenty-Four

Friday, September 14—Let's Make a Deal

Luca's days were busy with writing the chapters his editor wanted and keeping an eye on the various businesses he'd invested in. He was also thinking about another business he wanted to start. Then, there was the matter of collaborating with Arnold on the rebuild of Joy's garage. He was exhausted at the end of every day. Unfortunately, once he settled into bed at night, worry over Eric's future settled in. Michael Knight seemed too confident. What could he and Daniel possibly have up their sleeves to take Eric away from them? Why would Daniel, of all people, want to do this? He'd made his feelings about the boy clear.

Through the door of his study, he spotted Joy coming back from a day of job hunting. She looked as tired as he felt. He wished the woman would take a little time to get past the destruction of the salon. She'd refused the money he'd offered her for her bills. As a matter of fact, he'd thought she was going to strangle him when he'd suggested it. She had one hundred percent pride and zero percent savings. And as he'd feared, she was under-insured…again.

"Can you come in for a minute, Joy?" he called out. "There's something I'd like to show you."

Joy staggered in the office and melted into a chair at the front of his desk.

"Can I have Mrs. Washington bring you a glass of iced tea, or would you rather have something from the bar?"

"Just fill the bathtub with cold water and give me a straw." While he filled a glass with ice and water, she continued, "No one simply hires a stylist anymore. They rent their booths out. I can't afford that. The ones who are looking for a full-time person require you to have a good, local client list. Everyone I've ever worked on lives in Summer Springs. I'm afraid I'll have to start waiting tables or cashier at a store. Once I move back home, I'll have to drive back and forth. There's another expense."

"I have a better idea." Luca handed her a package of printed pictures in an envelope and watched her eyes widen as she looked through them. He'd taken several shots of each room in a large, high-end salon. It had a spacious waiting area, four styling booths, two shampoo sinks, a room set up for nail care, and another for waxing.

"This place is gorgeous. Where is it? Are they hiring?"

He tapped the stack of pictures in her hand. "They're selling out, and I'm thinking of buying it— that is if you agree to run it. You can make the hiring decisions or rent the spaces like you say others do."

Joy suddenly looked furious. "You don't need a salon. You're just trying to create a job for me. You think I'll never find a job on my own."

He handed her a list from the top drawer of his desk. "I knew you were going to say that. So, I got this ready. These are the other businesses I've invested in. When I see a profitable opportunity, I take it. Not all my money comes from writing books."

Joy tried to hand the list back to him, but he held up both hands to refuse it.

"To answer your other question about location, it's on the main highway between here and Summer Springs, near shopping and restaurants. You should let your Summer Springs customers know that. They could make the trip easily and spend the day pampering themselves."

Joy shook her head. "I'm just a stylist. I've never worked in a place this large, let alone managed one."

"You could still work on clients and run the business however you think best. All I'd recommend is putting a coffee and juice bar in the waiting area. I'll provide the start-up money; we'll split the profits—after your salary as manager of course. Should I apply for the permits and have a partnership contract written up? I like the name *Southern Style*. We could keep that. You can do this, Joy. I know you can."

Joy narrowed her eyes in suspicion. "There has to be a catch. Why is the shop being sold?"

He grinned. "The lady who owns it now has decided to relocate to Miami. Personally, I think that's a mistake on her part, but whatever. The fixtures and equipment are practically new. I talked her into selling those as well. If you want to hold onto the pictures and think about it for a few days, I understand." He came around the desk to lean over her with a hand on each arm of her chair. His voice dropped to a whisper. "I could give you a kiss to help you think about it. If you decide to take me up on my offer, we could seal the deal with something a whole lot nicer."

She whispered back, "I'm not sure kisses would help me think of anything other than the whole lot nicer."

He moved closer. "You have no idea how much that turns me on."

"Sir." Nelson appeared in the doorway.

Luca shot up arrow straight and turned toward him. "Yes, Nelson?"

"Your car insurance company called. I took the liberty of providing them with the police department case number. They said they should be back in touch with you soon."

"That's fine, Nelson, but I didn't expect you to be home this early. Doesn't Eric have an appointment with Doctor Johnson this evening?"

Nelson looked a little uncomfortable when he stepped closer. "Yes, I believe he does. I still take Eric to school every morning, sir, but I've been relieved of the duty to bring him home afterward."

"How does he get home from school?"

Nelson looked back and forth between him and Joy. "It seems he rides the bus to Miss Sullivan's house as he did before the fire. Then, Arnold drives him home."

Joy tilted her head, confused. "Why would he do that?"

Nelson cleared his throat before saying, "I believe it has something to do with Miss Janet."

Luca's eyes flew to Joy who looked just as surprised. "I've noticed he gets home later than he used to. Does Arnold have him working on the garage?"

"No, sir." Nelson shifted his feet. "Arnold takes

Bryce Foster home before they return here. Sometimes they stay a few extra minutes."

Luca shook his head. "He and Bryce have certainly become good friends. But why does Arnold let him hang around over there when he knows he has homework to do?"

Nelson stretched his neck and tried desperately to hold back a grin. "Well, sir, I believe that has something to do with Miss Foster."

Luca and Joy now looked at each other with expressions of mixed amazement and amusement. After a few seconds, they both folded in laughter.

"Arnold has the hots for Bryce's mom?" Luca asked when he caught his breath.

Nelson replied with a rare smile. "I've heard the feeling is mutual, sir."

As soon as he left the room, Mugsy pranced in.

Luca groaned. "Can't we get just a minute of privacy?"

"I don't think he'll tell on us." Joy laughed.

****

Dr. Johnson leafed through the few pages Eric had handed him. "What happened with your journal this week?"

Eric had expected that question. "It's been a rough one, Doc. Aunt Joy's shop was set on fire, and we had to move into Uncle Luca's house. It's a nice house, but Aunt Joy is super stressed."

The doctor gasped. "I imagine she is. Was anyone hurt?"

"Thanks for not asking if I did it," Eric said sincerely. "The cops put me in handcuffs right off. Luckily, I was with my friend, Bryce. He was my alibi.

They questioned all of us. This detective thinks it may have been the same guy who sabotaged my parent's plane and who blew up Uncle Luca's old house. I guess we're all pretty stressed."

Dr. Johnson had stopped taking notes and leaned forward. "Are you afraid for your safety?"

Eric picked at the rubber around the sole of his shoe. "I am kind of scared, but not because of all that. Something else is going on now. Like we needed another thing to worry about."

"What is it?"

Eric felt a lump form in his throat. "My grandfather, Grand-Dan, has decided he's going to fight my aunt and uncle both for guardianship of me. He says he's my real next of kin, and I guess he doesn't care what my mom or dad wanted."

The doctor laid his notepad aside. "Would that be a bad thing? He is your grandfather."

Eric nodded. "I'm not usually allowed in the house, but I went over there with Uncle Luca a couple of weeks ago. He called me a criminal and a crook. He was afraid I'd steal the stupid silver. And then he implied that I had something to do with my parents' deaths. Can you believe that? The guy really hates me...and I'm not crazy about him, either. I'd rather die than have to go with him. He'll send me to that teen boot-camp school in Samoa for rich juvenile delinquents. They tried to get my dad to send me there...him and my great-grandfather."

"Are you serious, Eric?"

"If I'm lying, I'm dying, Doc."

Dr. Johnson sat with his head down for a minute before he took a business card from his shirt pocket. He scribbled his personal cell phone number on the back. "I don't ever do this, Eric, but I want you to put this number in your phone. If you ever need help, call me. I'm on your side—and so are your aunt and uncle. Anybody can see that."

Eric nodded his head and slipped the card into the front pocket of his jeans.

"You can go home early today. I want some extra time to write my report to Judge Benedict. Don't worry about the missing pages in your journal. He'll understand."

Eric stood. "I appreciate that, Doc. I've got a monster problem with my homework. Give the Judge-Your Honor-Sir my regards."

Chapter Twenty-Five

Saturday, September 15—Together We Stand

For the first time in a week, Joy slept through the night. She'd dreamed about the offer Luca had made the day before and about the beautiful salon he wanted to buy. Now, in the light of day, she felt apprehensive.

Could she really trust a Wolff? He was different from the other men in his family. But was the deal too good to be true? He showed her a list of businesses he said he'd backed. She'd recognized a few of the names. Perhaps she should look up their phone numbers and check it out. She'd never heard a word of scandal regarding Luca. That was saying a lot for someone in his tax bracket.

As she sat at the kitchen table, enjoying the first morning cup of coffee, she said, "What do you think, Mugsy?"

The little pup tilted his head as though he was considering her question.

Her mind suddenly snapped to Daniel Wolff and his threat to take Eric. The money didn't matter that much to her. It would have been nice, especially with Eric to consider, but she'd never been that lucky. She'd known better than to count on it. She wished it was only about the money.

Luca entered the room, Arnold close behind. He stopped by the sideboard to pour himself a cup of coffee. "What's making you look so glum this morning?"

Arnold stopped to scratch Mugsy behind the ears. "I'm afraid I don't have the kind of news that'll make you any happier, Miss Joy."

She lifted her hands in the air. "Okay, I always like to start the day with bad news. Go ahead and ruin my morning, Arnold."

After a brief moment of hesitation, he said, "I've got all the debris cleared away at your house and inspected the situation fully. Sorry to say, you'll need new wiring and insulation in that wall between the house and garage. I think it would be wise to replace the wires all the way to the circuit box in the whole living room and kitchen." He made a cup of coffee for himself and sat across from her. "Of course, the drywall will have to be replaced as well. The smoke smell in the furniture and carpeting is bad. I'd recommend you replace that, as well. The kitchen furniture is okay, and the cabinets can probably be taken care of with a good cleaning and paint job. Here's the deal: Eric, Bryce, and I can do a lot of the work ourselves, but the insurance isn't going to cover it all."

Luca looked annoyed. "Why are you bothering Miss Sullivan about this? You know I can take care of the difference."

"I told him not to do that," Joy informed him. "You're already providing the man power. I'll just have to make the money stretch."

Arnold cleared his throat. "I don't know if you'll still feel that way when I give you the bottom line, Miss

Sullivan."

"Why? How bad is it?"

The handyman continued. "There's the stuff I already told you about, but I can finish the job with the money you have if I cap off the plumbing and electricity to the area and build a carport in that place. I'd be willing to put in some really pretty landscaping around it free of charge."

"Well." Joy raised her chin to keep tears from filling her eyes. Her only source of income for the last ten years had literally gone up in flames. Mugsy growled. "I guess that's what we'll have to do then."

"Do you have any good news?" Luca asked with a measure of sarcasm.

Arnold nodded. "Actually, I do. There was a firewall between the house and garage that saved the attic area."

Joy expected that to be the case. "The garage had been a late addition to the house. The old owners built it to raise the value of the house."

A smile crept onto Luca's lips. "Do you know what I think?"

She didn't feel like talking about his business offer right now. She just wanted to wallow in self-pity for a few minutes.

"I think Arnold is looking for a way to stick around Summer Springs longer. What do you suppose he finds so attractive in that area? Could it possibly be a woman with a teenaged son? He did include Bryce in his plans."

His playful banter put a smile on her face as well…and a blush on Arnold's. He looked more like a teenager, at that moment, than a man in his thirties.

"That kind of brings me to a question I wanted to ask, sir."

Luca rolled his eyes. "Yes, you have my permission to ask for the lady's hand in marriage."

Arnold's thick, dark mustache twitched, but he took on a serious expression. "I was thinking more along the line of a picnic and fishing tomorrow. Bryce will be there, so I wondered if Eric could come along, too. They could keep each other busy while we…talk."

Luca gasped and turned to Joy. "That would give the grown-ups alone time. Imagine the possibilities!"

Arnold grinned. "It sounds like you have a few romantic ideas of your own."

"To be honest," Luca replied, "I was thinking about an afternoon nap by the pool without the sounds of rap music and video games."

Eric entered and flopped onto a chair at the end of the table. Mugsy ran to him, barking until he was lifted into the boy's lap. "Are you talking about my birthday party? I wanted to ask—would next weekend be good for you guys or the weekend after. My actual birthday falls in the middle of the week."

Luca huffed. "Yeah, in a couple of months. Why do we have to decide now?"

Eric quirked a brow. "What have you been smoking, dude? My birthday is September twenty-seventh. That's only twelve days from today."

Joy nodded her head. "It's true. I was sitting in the hospital waiting room when he was born. I'll never forget how loud he howled. You could hear him all the way down the hall."

"That can't be," Luca frowned. "I was in my first tour to the Middle East. We had just sat down for

Thanksgiving dinner when I got the call. It was November twenty-seventh. I wrote it down."

Eric laughed, and Mugsy barked his agreement. "Somebody's trippin'. I have a birth certificate if you want to know who."

"No, that's okay."

Joy was concerned about the confusion in Luca's expression. Why would he have gotten the call two months after Eric's birth? He had to be mistaken.

"We'll have the party next weekend," Luca announced. "Bring a list of your demands to my office this afternoon."

****

Luca had just shut down his computer for the day when Eric walked into his office with a loose-leaf binder under his arm. "Does that whole thing contain plans for your party?"

"No." He took a folded piece of lined paper from the front pocket of his pants. "I found a place where we can rent a few arcade-style games, a popcorn machine, and a soda machine. We can order the pizzas, and Mrs. Washington said she'd take care of the cake and ice cream. You have a good enough sound system, but I get to pick the music."

"How many people are you inviting?"

"I have a few new acquaintances now that I'm hanging around with Bryce. I'd say around twelve or fifteen. Janet said she'd bring a few girls to even things out."

Luca looked at the address and phone number of the rental company. "Seems simple enough."

Joy came in with Mugsy at her heels. "I heard that you've been spending a little time with Janet. I guess it's all about that Wolff charm."

Eric sighed. "The only Wolff who may have a little charm is Uncle Luca, and he's never been married. I think Janet just hangs around us because of Bryce."

"Has she said that?" Joy asked.

Eric shook his head and reached for the dog. "No, but I figure she likes big guys. She was going out with Mitch Frazier when school started. He's a huge butthead. I'm glad she dumped him."

Luca had an idea. "I think you should plan to have your party out by the pool. That way the girls can see how you've toned up your muscles since you started working out. Also, you can see them in their bathing suits—an added bonus."

A smile spread across Eric's face. "I like the way you think, old man."

Luca gave the kid a pass on the old man comment. "So, why did you bring that ragged-looking binder in here?"

"I have a problem with a project I'm doing for American History. It's a study on our family tree. The idea is to show us how we all started as immigrants from other countries and combined cultures, languages, religions, and races."

Joy looked at the book from over his shoulder. "That makes sense."

"Not to Henry Nighthawk. He's a guy in my class whose family has been in the country since the beginning of time—so he says." Eric told her.

Luca rolled his eyes. "Okay, but what's the problem you're having?"

"We used the ancestry program from a website. I sent for a DNA analysis and entered all the information in great-grandma's old bible. My DNA chart and my family tree don't match. The tree doesn't show the Italian part of my family that comes up in my DNA."

Joy held up a hand to stop him. "Those things aren't always accurate. A friend of mine knew her family was French. They even had a French last name. But they were listed as German when they entered the United States. On further investigation, she found out her grandfather's family had fled France under the threat of religious persecution. They sailed out of Germany for this country, and no one asked where they'd originally come from."

Luca took the binder. "That makes perfect sense. When does this project have to be turned in?"

"It's not really due until the end of the semester, but I wanted to get it over with sooner."

"Why don't you leave it with me? I have a few connections that would be helpful with this."

Luca put the binder on the credenza behind him and then turned to Joy. "Have you come to give me an answer to what we talked about yesterday?"

She shrugged. "Not really, but I guess I have to say yes, after the information I got this morning from Arnold."

Eric looked excited. "Answer to what? What did you talk about yesterday?"

"Just a minute." Luca lifted a finger in his direction. "I don't want you to say yes because you have to. I want you to say yes because it's an exciting proposal. I want you to be happy with this decision."

Eric dramatically dropped to his knees. "Come on, you guys. You're killing me."

"I think it can work," Joy told Luca. "I am happy."

"Partners then?" Luca held his hand out, and Joy shook it.

"Partners."

Eric groaned. "Is anybody going to tell me what's going on here?"

Luca turned to face Eric. "Your aunt Joy and I have decided to go into business together. We're opening a new salon."

Eric stood up and hunched his shoulders. "Way to let a guy down, you two."

Joy watched him drop into a chair to cuddle Mugsy. "What do you suppose he means by that?"

"Who knows. He's a teenager." Luca stealthily hid an old napkin he'd held onto for almost fifteen years. The one he'd written Eric's name and birth date on the day he'd been told the boy had been born. "If you're concerned about what I said to Eric this morning, I think I must have made a mistake. It may have been my cousin who called that Thanksgiving. She had a baby that year, too."

Joy snapped her fingers. "I almost forgot. I just got a call from Barbara Allgood."

Luca saw a crease between her eyes. "You don't look happy about that."

"She said the judge's office called. He must have received the papers. He wants to see us in his chambers on Thursday afternoon."

Luca threw up his hands. "So soon, and here I am without an attorney."

"You're not the only one," Joy stated. "Barbara told me she thinks she's gotten in over her head. I guess you could say—she dumped me."

Eric plucked the party plans off Luca's desk. "So

much for a happy birthday. I may be celebrating in Samoa."

"No way." Luca snatched the paper out of his hand. "The party is in a week. Start inviting people.

"I will not give up. I won't let either of you give up. This crazy mess threw the three of us together, and dammit, we're going to stick together. It only took one little boy to slay a giant. Together we can surely take out a couple of assholes."

Late that night, Luca called Nelson to his room. "Do you still have contact with those special friends of yours?"

Nelson straightened his vest. "Of course, sir. Is there a problem you need looked into?"

"Yes. You know my brother claims to have some kind of ammunition to take Eric away from me."

"I'm aware of that. Have you found out what that ammunition is?"

Luca told him about the confusion regarding Eric's birthday. He showed him the actual napkin he'd written the date on and tucked away in his notebook all those years ago. It definitely included Eric's name. He showed him the ancestry DNA chart Eric had sent for and how it drastically differed from the family tree. "I don't know how Daniel plans to use this information to his advantage, but I suspect Eric isn't David's biological child."

Nelson compared the materials. "It would be easy enough to find out. The tissue samples that were taken from David and his wife would still be at the lab in Tampa. All I need is a little sample from Eric. I'll get that first thing in the morning. He won't know a thing.

"Have you considered the possibility that the boy

was slipped in by adoption? You were out of the country."

"Joy said she was at the hospital when Melissa gave birth. Have her tissue tested as well though. It seems farfetched, but kids have been switched in hospital nurseries."

"Leave it to me, sir. I'll have an answer to you as soon as possible."

Luca ran his fingers through his hair. "I hope so. There's no telling what Judge Benedict is going to do Thursday. I'll try to hold him off from making any final decisions for as long as I can."

Chapter Twenty-Six

Thursday, September 20—Preparations

Joy stared at herself in the mirror. Melissa would love the way she looked, but it was a far stretch from what she was used to.

Luca had taken her shopping on Sunday to pick out a suit for today. He had a perfect eye for style. Her jacket was emerald green with large black buttons and a wide black lapel. It was paired with a black pencil skirt which had a small slit at the back hem. The shoes were plain black pumps with a wedge heel about three inches high. He'd said he didn't want her breaking an ankle going up the courthouse steps.

While she'd tried the suit on, he'd chosen a pair of chunky black earrings. He didn't want her to wear any other jewelry. The idea was to show they meant business when they faced his brother in the judge's chambers.

For the first time in her life, she'd spent nearly an hour on her makeup. It was slightly dramatic without looking over the top. Her hair was slicked back into a high twist. Her nails were French-tipped, but not too long. She pressed a hand over her nervous stomach.

"What do you think, Mugsy?" She laughed when he gave a sharp bark of approval.

She checked the square black handbag to make sure it contained a compact and lipstick, her wallet and keys, a roll of hard cherry candies, and a package of tissue. What would she do for the next hour?

That question was answered a moment later when Mrs. Washington tapped on her door. "I know you haven't eaten a bite of food today."

"My stomach is jumping like a bunny with its tail on fire. I don't know if I could keep anything down."

The older woman walked into the room carrying a small tray. "I figured as much. I brought you a cup of warm tea and a few crackers. You don't want your belly to grumble at the wrong time."

Joy sat at the dressing table and sipped the tea. "You think of everything," she sighed. "I think Luca must love the color green. He bought me a green car, now this suit."

Mrs. Washington chuckled. "Actually, his favorite color is red. He just likes green on you. I think it's your eyes. I see the way he looks at you when you're not aware."

Joy blushed, but it was more from the memory of a few stolen kisses than Mrs. Washington's observations. Still, it felt pretty incredible to hear. "I think you're making more of it than there is. He could have any woman he wanted. I'm sure there's been a long list."

Mrs. Washington gathered damp towels from the adjoining bathroom. "He's not the playboy type, you know. The only time he asks a woman out is when he attends a function he can't avoid. As long as I've known him you're the first single, female guest he's had in his home overnight. He's a very solitary creature. And that's all the gossiping I'll bother you with."

There were times when Mrs. Washington sounded more like Luca's mother than his housekeeper. "Thank you, Mrs. Washington. You've been so nice to me and made me feel at home here."

"Well"—the older woman smiled—"maybe one day you'll see your way clear to sharing that meatloaf recipe."

"Absolutely."

Joy felt much better when she went to find Eric.

He stepped out of his room looking as stunning as his uncle in a black-and-gray-striped dress shirt. The sleeves were folded back to his elbows, and the tail tucked neatly into black jeans. He'd traded his cross trainers for a pair of leather boots. He'd even styled his hair away from his face. The light fuzz was gone from his chin. He'd shaved. Was he old enough to shave?

Eric looked her up and down, nodding his approval. "You look like you just stepped out of a perfume commercial."

"Is that good?" Joy asked.

He took her hand and began leading her toward the study. "That's excellent. Uncle Luca's eyes are going to bug out when he sees you. He told me to come in so he could see what I look like. I want to be there when he gets a load of you." Before she could turn back, Eric was opening the door.

Luca stood by the window in a silver-gray suit and shoes which were the same color. His black shirt was collarless with the top button undone. He looked incredible. When he turned and saw her he didn't say a word. He just nodded stiffly. "Eric, do you have your wallet and phone?"

Eric patted his pockets. "I do."

"Be sure you have your phone silenced before we get there," Luca reminded the boy. "Did you shave the way I told you to?"

Eric gave him a sloppy salute. "Yes, sir."

"You look good." Luca finished.

Eric's mouth dropped open. "That's it? Aren't you going to say something about how Aunt Joy looks?"

"Yes—I am—as soon as you give us a little privacy."

"Oh!" Eric looked back and forth between them with wide eyes. "I guess I can do that."

As soon as the door closed behind her nephew, Luca looped one arm around her waist. His other hand cupped the nape of her neck to pull her into the most passionate kiss she'd experienced so far. After a few powerful heartbeats, he pulled away. "I hadn't planned to do that. You're just so damned gorgeous." He sat behind his desk and motioned to the chair across from him. "I have to talk to you—now more than ever."

Nerves prickled at the back of Joy's neck. What now? "Is something wrong?"

"Not so far, but just hear me out." He took a deep breath and rubbed his fingers over his forehead. "I think you know I'm extremely attracted to you. We've had chemistry between us since the day we met. I'd like to explore that more, a lot more.

"Also, there's the matter of the new salon. I've closed on the sale and have the partnership contract drawn up. But I think we should wait until this problem with Eric's guardianship is resolved.

"I'm not saying I've changed my mind about anything. I know what I want. But now that my brother is involved, this fight could get nasty. I'm not sure if you realize just how nasty it may be. I don't know how you're going to feel about me when the smoke clears. I don't want you to feel like you're trapped into something you regret if this mess goes south."

The prickly feeling ran down Joy's spine. "I feel like there's something you're not telling me."

Luca picked up a pen and nervously twirled it between his fingers. "I think you agree that Eric has to come before anything else. Whatever I say or do will be to protect him, even if it causes some pain. I would expect the same from you."

She moved to the edge of the chair. "Of course, I agree. I'd do anything for Eric. But you're scaring me a little."

After a pause, Luca took a deep breath and continued, "I'm proposing that we keep a respectful distance from each other until we know exactly where we stand. And I want you to understand that I'm going to fight fire with fire. I will not allow my brother to get his hands on that boy. Hopefully, when this is over, we can pick up where we left off."

"You're worrying me, Luca."

"Please, just trust me."

Joy was completely confused. All he'd talked about was the new salon. And every time they were alone for a minute, he'd cornered her for a kiss. Now he'd cooled on both those things in what seemed like an instant. She was more anxious than before to find out what was going to happen today. Was he finally going to show his true Wolff colors?

****

Eric did a little dance as he entered the kitchen

smiling.

Nelson gazed over the rim of his teacup. "You look like the cat who ate the canary."

"Uncle Luca ran me off. He said he and Aunt Joy needed privacy."

The teacup clattered against its saucer when Nelson sat it aside. "Maybe they had to discuss something they didn't want you to hear."

"You're such a downer, Nelson." Eric popped open a Coke. Then, he helped himself to a hand full of popcorn from a tin on the counter. Nelson rolled his eyes when he dumped the popcorn on the bare table and sat down. "I think they're kissing, you know, like making out. This could turn into something big. Maybe we'll all be living here for real someday."

One brow lifted before Nelson replied, "Although I wouldn't object to its happening, I think you shouldn't get your hopes up. It could just be a brief flirtation or nothing at all. They're adults. We should mind our own business and just hope for the best for them both."

"You know, Nelson, I think this is going to be a great day. I can feel it in my bones."

Nelson stood and straightened his vest. "I think it's just the new clothes talking, Master Eric. By the way, don't forget to wipe down the table and brush the popcorn out of your teeth before you leave...sir."

Chapter Twenty-Seven

Thursday, September 20—A United Front

When Luca guided Joy and Eric to the door of Judge Benedict's chamber, they were met by a security guard. "The judge asked me to direct you to the conference room down the hall." The uniformed man pointed to a door across the hall and two rooms to the left. "He said he can't contain a crowd here."

Luca remembered the judge's chamber as a comfortable and spacious room. "What does he mean a crowd?"

The guard looked straight ahead and let his hands fall to his sides. "Don't ask me, sir. I'm just the messenger."

When he opened the other door, he understood. Judge Benedict sat at the head of a large oak table. At his right, Michael Knight sat between his father and brother. Three empty chairs waited on his left. However, they still had the advantage of numbers.

Larry Meyers and Dr. Johnson sat in the back corner. Luca felt the urge to growl at Johnson when he looked Joy up and down, but he let it slide. They could use all the help they could get. Both men stood with smiling faces and waited for them to take their places.

Knight appeared irritated. "Your Honor, I thought

this was going to be a closed meeting. You've already talked to Miss Sullivan and Luca Wolff. My client should have the opportunity to have your attention now."

The judge glared at him with tight lips. "Who I invite to this meeting is my prerogative, counselor. And I'd like to add, I don't have much respect for an attorney who switches sides in the middle of a case. I'm not altogether sure I'm going to allow it."

"I haven't switched sides, sir. I've worked for the Wolff family for over five years. I'm representing Daniel Wolff because I feel it's in the best interest of the child."

Luca was proud of the way Eric kept his cool when he'd been referred to as a child.

Judge Benedict snickered, but he didn't look amused. "In his best interest or your bank account's best interest? Don't bother answering that." The judge pointed to Meyers and Johnson. "As far as these gentlemen being here, they've been court appointed. Do you have a problem with that?"

Knight's cheeks reddened. "I don't see that I have a choice, Your Honor."

The judge slapped the table top to indicate the meeting would begin. "Since we have four men in the room with the same last name, I'll call you by your first names. Is that agreeable?" When no one objected he continued. "Daniel Wolff, can you explain to me why you've decided to challenge your brother and Miss Sullivan for custody of Eric?"

Daniel cleared his throat and tugged at the top of his tie. "Your Honor, I'm sure my son never imagined I would outlive him. It's a fact I'm having a hard time coming to terms with it myself. But if he could, I know he'd agree that, as Eric's next of kin, I would be the best person to raise the boy. I also feel that any money David and Melissa left behind should go to Eric. As his rightful guardian, I should be the executor of those funds."

The judge straightened in his seat. "That was a remarkable jump to the money, Daniel. Your daughter-in-law clearly decided her sister would be best for Eric. Why do you suppose she felt that way?"

"Melissa was a hopeless and bitter alcoholic, sir." Luca saw Joy flinch from the corner of his eye. Eric, sitting between them, took her hand. Daniel continued, "She was in the process of divorcing my son. The woman made her will naming her sister as sole beneficiary and Eric's guardian as an insult to our family. I don't believe she was in her right mind. Her will should be ignored."

Judge Benedict shifted in his seat looking uncomfortable and angry. "I believe it's my job to decide what will be ignored, Mister Wolff. Can you tell me why you think you'd be a better guardian than either of the two people across from you?"

Daniel answered, "That's obvious, Your Honor. I have the needed experience. I've already raised one respectable, well adjusted, and successful son. There's no question about that."

"It's Eric we're talking about now." The judge hit the table. "I was the person who broke the news to him that his parents had perished two weeks earlier. Where were you? Why hadn't you talked to him? You said, in front of witnesses, that he was your grandson and you'd take care of it."

The confidence drained from Daniel's expression. "I was grieving, Your Honor. I wasn't thinking. I'd just lost my son."

The judge spoke between clenched teeth. "Eric had lost both parents. Don't you think he had a right to grieve as well?"

Daniel stammered before saying, "Of course. It was a horrible time for all of us. But I must insist, sir, neither of these people have the experience or resources I have to raise a boy properly. I did a good job with David. He was loyal to the family. He took his proper place in Wolff Enterprises and didn't run off to kill people and write idiotic books about it."

The judge didn't relent. "I've read those books. They aren't idiotic. I admire your brother for his bravery and devotion to his country."

The oldest Wolff made a harrumph sound as he sat back and crossed his arms.

"Gerald Wolff, you are the one who confuses me most," the judge sneered. "Why have you sided with one son against the other?"

Gerald appeared happy to have his say. "Like Daniel, I want what's best for the boy. Luca is as high-strung, disrespectful, and ill-tempered as his mother. I regret letting her have her way with him. I should have taken him from her the day she left. He wasn't raised in the proper environment I could have provided.

"It would be even worse for the boy to grow up in Miss Sullivan's home. Trash only breeds more trash. I have no doubt she's just like her cheating, lying mother. The woman had no morals whatsoever."

Luca saw Eric put his arm around Joy's shoulder. He wished he could be beside her to comfort her. More than that, he wished he could fly across the table, strangle his father, and flatten Daniel's nose.

The judge slumped back into his seat. "It sounds like a debate of nature versus nurture. What do you think, Dr. Johnson?"

All eyes turned to the end of the table where Johnson sat. "In my opinion, there is no real answer to that question. Every individual reacts differently. One family can happily raise several well-adjusted children, but one of those children may grow up to be a serial killer. However, Eric is the topic of discussion today.

"He was a rude, crude, extremely sad boy when I met him. Since living with Luca Wolff and Miss Sullivan, he's made a one-hundred-eighty-degree turn. He's been given responsibilities and takes pride in doing good work. He thinks of others instead of himself, as he did before. He's happy. I think both of his current guardians have done a great job."

The judge pointed to Eric's social worker. "What do you say, Mr. Meyers?"

"I have to agree with Bennett. I've talked to Eric's teachers and a few of his friends. His change of attitude over the last few weeks has been remarkable. As you can see, he cares deeply for his aunt and admires his uncle. To force him to give either of them up would be traumatizing."

"I agree," the judge stated. "However, I can't disregard the fact that Daniel Wolff is his nearest relation."

Luca couldn't stay quiet for another minute. "He doesn't even allow Eric in his house, Your Honor. He plans to send him to a school for delinquent rich kids over in Samoa. He may as well be a POW."

"Is this true?" the judge asked Daniel.

Daniel smirked. "I wondered how long it would take for my brother to lose control. There's something you should know, Your Honor. Luca suffers from PTSD. Eric is in danger, just being close to him."

"How dare you," Joy blurted. "You don't know anything about what he's been through while you sat at a desk getting fat on your family's money."

Doctor Johnson raised a pen to take the floor. "I'd be willing to evaluate Mister Wolff's mental state, sir. But if PTSD made a person too dangerous to raise a child, we'd have to take children away from hundreds of American veterans, rape victims, and anyone else who's ever suffered trauma."

Michael Knight interrupted. "I'm not surprised by Miss Sullivan's behavior, Your Honor. If you want to argue about nature versus nurture, she's your example for the nature side. For years, the people around town have speculated about who her mother had cavorted with to give birth to a biracial child. I have the answer to that question." He proudly held up a manila folder. "This is a statement from a vicious criminal in the Florida State Prison. He has sworn to the fact that he was Mr. Sullivan's gardener and Mrs. Sullivan's lover at the time she became pregnant for Joy. According to him, Miss Sullivan's mother was an eager partner in the relationship." He handed the folder to the judge. "These are not the kind of people who should be raising an already troubled boy. I think it would be best for Eric to come home with his grandfather today…for his own safety."

As Joy appeared to be in shock, Luca sprung to his feet. "Would you be so anxious to claim Eric if you found out he isn't a Wolff?" he asked Daniel. "I have reason to believe that Eric isn't David's son. I didn't want to say anything until the tests are completed. Melissa was pregnant before they were married. A DNA test has put his paternity in question."

The room fell silent until Gerald Wolff stood to face the judge. "If this is true, I don't want anything to do with the little bastard."

"If it's true," Daniel added. "I want any consideration for him removed from my son's will."

"This meeting is over," Judge Benedict bellowed. "Eric will return to Miss Sullivan's care until further notice. While we wait for these test results, I'll take everything said in this room under careful consideration."

"Your Honor," Knight exclaimed.

The judge hit the table again. "Shut up, Knight. You make me sick."

Luca waited outside the ladies' room until Joy composed herself, then followed her and Eric from the building. He stopped them on the steps. "I'm sorry, Joy. I tried to make you understand how bad this was going to be."

She threw open the glass door and stepped outside as the others followed. "It was bad when they implied my mother was a whore, but you had to paint Melissa with the same brush. That was what I didn't expect. Personally, I don't care who Eric's father is. I don't even care who mine is. I never needed him, and I don't need you. I intend to go back to my own life and put it back in order."

"I guess I have to be understanding of that, but I still want to help with Eric's expenses. He'll always be family to me, and so will you…no matter how this turns out."

When Joy turned to walk away, Luca grabbed Eric's shoulder.

"You know I love you, don't you kid? I'm sorry for everything that went down in there. I didn't want you to find out this way."

"I guess." Eric shrugged.

"Take care of your Aunt Joy. She needs you. Dammit, we all need each other."

"Are you going to be all right?"

Eric couldn't have said anything to make Luca more proud. "Yeah, man, I'll be okay. And I'll see you soon. The party is still on at my house on Saturday, don't forget." They hugged and gave each other a manly pat on the back before parting.

"Sir, I have news." Nelson ran toward Luca up the steps, when a shot rang out. His eyes widened in shock as a red mist sprayed from the upper right section of his suit jacket.

Luca grabbed Nelson to keep him from falling down the steps. Eric dove to cover Joy.

Chapter Twenty-Eight

Friday, September 21—A House Divided

At eight o'clock the next morning, Joy entered the waiting room with Mrs. Washington and Arnold. The night before, they'd stayed at the hospital until the doctor came out to inform them Nelson was in recovery and the surgery had been successful. Luca refused to leave. Now, she found him sleeping in a chair against the back wall. The jacket of his beautiful suit was wadded into a fake pillow and stuffed behind his neck. His eyes shot open the minute they entered the room.

"Has there been any news?" She handed Luca a travel mug of coffee and a container holding two large blueberry muffins. "I didn't figure you'd leave for food."

He yawned and then breathed the aroma from the mug. "You're right, I'm starved. Thank you." He took a sip and sighed. "I'm glad you're here. Nelson is still sleeping. Did Eric go to school?"

Joy sat beside him and nodded. "We had a terrible time getting him to cooperate, but Arnold promised to bring him here as soon as school lets out."

"Good. I want the whole family together."

Joy looked down at her folded hands. "Luca, I meant what I said at the courthouse. When Arnold told

Sandra Dailey

me the house had been approved for occupancy, I packed Eric's and my things up. They're in my car. We're moving back to Summer Springs today."

Luca set the muffins on a magazine table beside him. "I don't want you to leave."

She smiled sadly. "Consider it keeping a *respectful distance*."

"I guess I deserved that." Luca sipped his coffee. "About Melissa—you have to know I cared for her, too. David and I hung out with her and her friends a lot in our last two years of high school. We partied together in our first couple years of college. I went into the Marine Corps after that, and a few months later, they announced they were getting married. I didn't think it was a good idea. She had issues."

Joy wished she could grab the coffee from his hand and throw it. How dare he insult her sister? "Melissa was just as good as any Wolff ever born."

"I know you loved and admired your older sister, but she may not have been as angelic as you thought. She was wild. I don't think she ever got past her father leaving the way he did. I think she was trying to fill that void. She needed male attention—a lot of it. Can you understand?"

Joy felt a lump growing in her throat. "Were you among the males who gave her attention?"

"Yes," he admitted. "I was as young, wild, and stupid, like the others. We drank too much alcohol, smoked too much weed, and slept around. It's pretty embarrassing to even think about now."

"It wasn't that long ago."

"It feels like a lifetime ago, to me. I've built a good life for myself since then, but I've left out a few things along the way. I don't want to lose you and Eric."

Joy looked him in the eye to see his reaction. "Even if Eric isn't a Wolff?"

Luca sighed and gave her a weak smile. "That's only a name. It doesn't matter to me anymore. I've given it a lot of thought since we've had Eric. The Wolff name has given me more pain than pride. Eric would agree with me about that. What made me who I am are my experiences. What determines how I care for another person are the experiences we've shared. Look at my bond with Nelson. He's more important to me than my own father because of our philosophical conversations over a few glasses of cognac. David was my best friend, not because of the blood that ran through our veins, but the hours we spent riding bikes and chasing girls together. Eric and I are collecting some great experiences now." Luca shook his head. "I figure Melissa and David lied to me about his date of birth because they knew I'd guess the truth, but it wouldn't have made any difference to me."

Joy watched Luca pick up the bag Mrs. Washington had brought him and walk down the hall to find a place to clean up. He'd given her a lot to think about. She thumbed through a magazine without looking at a single page. She thought about the experiences she'd shared with her mother and Melissa. Then, she thought about experiences they hadn't shared. She'd always blamed Melissa's father for the situation he'd left her mother in, but they'd all made the best of it. It had never occurred to her how Melissa could be emotionally affected by his absence. He'd simply disappeared from her life and never returned. Melissa hadn't done anything to deserve his abandonment. This had all been *her* fault. Now, Eric was paying the price.

She watched Luca return from the men's room looking fresher after shaving and changing into a pair of blue jeans, sneakers, and an olive-green Henley shirt. Why did it hurt so much to find out he'd been with her sister? It was years ago. She and Luca only had a few kisses…hot, passionate kisses.

He sat between Mrs. Washington and Arnold. Their three heads came together as they whispered in what looked like an in-depth discussion. She wasn't part of that family. It wasn't any of her business. Just as she was about to leave, Detective Anderson entered the room with a uniformed officer.

****

"Mr. Wolff, could you please come across the hall where I can ask you a few questions?"

Luca followed him to a room with a sign that said Family Room. He'd expected inquiries to start before now.

The three men sat at a small round table in the corner. The uniformed officer took a note pad and pen from his shirt pocket without speaking a word.

Anderson folded his hands and leaned toward Luca. "Mr. Wolff, what can you tell me about Nelson Griffin?"

"I met Nelson ten years ago. We were both in a hospital in Saudi Arabia. I'd been flown there after taking a bullet in the shoulder. He was recovering from a shot to the hip. We were the only men in the room not interested in blowing our paychecks playing poker. In exchange for wheeling him outside, he offered to share a bottle of cognac with me.

"He told me about being trained by his father as a butler or, as he put it, a man's man. His family had served a wealthy family in southern England for generations until that family lost all their money. That's how he ended up in military service. He was afraid he'd be discharged and didn't know what he'd do for a living. I'd already had two successful books and made some good investments, so I offered him a position whenever he needed it. He's been working for me ever since then."

Anderson tilted his head to one side. "Do you know if he had any enemies?"

Luca nodded. "He was working for British Intelligence during his time in service. I know he stays in touch with some of his contacts. Their job was to root out enemy leaders. It was dangerous at the time, but he hasn't mentioned any personal threat since being in my employ."

Anderson looked impressed by Nelson's background. "Why did he come to the courthouse yesterday?"

"I don't know. Nelson didn't have a chance to tell me before he was shot. He's been unconscious since he's been here."

"Who were the people closest to him on the courthouse steps?"

Luca answered this question as well. "Just me, Eric, and Miss Sullivan."

"Do you have any enemies, Mr. Wolff?"

Luca folded his arms over his chest. "Not that I'm aware of, but my house was blown up. You know about that."

The detective next asked him, "Do you have any

business partners?"

"Several," Luca replied. "I'll supply you with a list. There hasn't been any trouble on that front."

"Do you know where Mrs. Washington was at the time of the shooting?" Anderson asked.

"Absolutely," Luca replied. "She was at the grocery store. I called after the EMTs arrived. It had only taken them a few minutes to get there. She uses the store on Commonwealth Avenue. It's all the way across town from the courthouse. She had told me yesterday morning she'd go there to check on the order for Eric's birthday cake and pick up a few things for his party. I could hear the cash register in the background as we spoke."

Anderson nodded. "Where was Arnold Campbell?"

"He was visiting a friend, Miss Dinah Foster. I'll get her address and phone number for you when we're finished. She lives in Summer Springs. It was her day off, and he'd gone to help her with a few repairs she needed around her house."

The uniformed officer gave a curt nod as he continued writing.

Anderson narrowed his eyes. "Has anyone asked for a gift or loan of money?"

Luca said, "No, no one lately."

Anderson asked, "Have you fired anyone from your employment recently?"

Luca said, "No. I only have my personal staff. My business partners are responsible for their employees."

Anderson paused before asking, "Who would profit from your death, Mr. Wolff?"

Luca looked slightly surprised, but calmly answered, "As my will currently stands, Eric is my sole beneficiary."

"Thanks for your cooperation, Mr. Wolff." Anderson stood and shook Luca's hand. "I'd like you to go back to the waiting room and ask Miss Sullivan to come in."

****

Joy stopped at the door marked Family Room. She'd been brought here the last time her mother was in the hospital. It's were the doctor had told her, her mother wouldn't survive the night. Her hand shook as she opened the door.

Both Detective Anderson and the police officer stood until she was seated. The room had been redecorated since the last time she'd seen it, which helped calm her nerves. However, she was caught off guard by Anderson's first question. "Miss Sullivan, do you have any enemies or have you received any threats?"

"No, never," she answered.

Anderson continued, "Have you had any men approach you for dates or anything lately?"

She shook her head. "No."

Anderson folded his hands and leaned forward. "I understand that you'll be coming into a lot of money soon. Who stands to profit from your death, Miss Sullivan?"

"I don't have a will, and I doubt I'll need one. The Wolff family plans to take my inheritance as well as my nephew. I haven't told anyone about the inheritance, mostly because I doubt I'll ever see it."

Anderson's voice was gentler. "I don't think whatever is going on involves you, Miss Sullivan, but I'd like you to be cautious. You were close to Mr.

Griffin when he was shot. So were Eric and Luca Wolff. I'm going to ask patrols to ride by your house as often as possible."

Joy's face felt numb, but her heart was racing. She hadn't considered the danger to Eric. "Thank you, Detective."

****

Eric's nerves were still on edge as Arnold drove him to the hospital. He'd never seen a man shot, and this had been someone close to him. He was startled when Arnold spoke.

"I'm going to let you in on the plan, but you have to keep it covert. Can you do that?"

He wasn't sure he liked that idea. "You mean you don't want Aunt Joy to know what's going on. Why?"

Arnold glanced at him, and then turned his eyes back to the road. "I think your Aunt Joy is great, Eric, but she's not a team player. To be honest, she's as stubborn as a mule. She's never relied on anyone but herself. If she knew what we're doing, she'd refuse our help."

He was right. Eric nodded. "Okay, I get it. What's the plan?"

"She's already decided that the two of you are moving back to her house today."

His first thought was of Janet and Bryce. "Groovy! I'll be back with my buds!"

"Yeah, well, she's a little upset with your Uncle Luca right now. It's just one of those grown-up things. They'll get over it."

One of those grown-up things? He was tired of being treated like a child. "I know. It's about some things that came out in yesterday's meeting with the

222

judge and my grandfathers."

"He doesn't want her to be unprotected. Mrs. Washington is going to move with you."

Eric pictured the older woman with a rolling pin in her hand. "She's our protection?"

"She's one of the most kickass marines I know. The woman could hear an intruder before he even reached your block. She'd have him shot between the eyes before he could get out of his car. I'm not joking, kid. She's good."

The rolling pin in his mind turned into an assault rifle. "Awesome!"

"As far as your aunt is concerned, Mrs. Washington is mad at Luca and wants to help out while your aunt finds work. Mrs. Washington has an idea for that problem, as well."

It sounded like a decent enough plan. "Okay, anything else?"

"Yeah, you know that house across the street that's been empty for so long?"

Eric pictured the old gray house with its tall grass. "Yeah, where the old man died."

"Umm, yeah." Arnold turned into the hospital's parking area. "Me and your uncle are going to be staying there. Don't let your aunt find out, though. We'll be watching the house and make sure no one tries to put a bomb under the car or anything. Hopefully, we'll catch whoever killed your parents. You want to be part of that, don't you?"

Eric wanted to see the responsible person fry. "Sure, but what am I supposed to do?"

Arnold parked his truck but didn't move to open the door. "You act like you're taking the school bus as usual, but I'll be following. Don't take off like you have a couple times already. Stay at the house. Keep your eyes and ears open. If you want to see your friends, invite them to come to you—only Bryce or Janet though. I don't know the others. If Bryce needs a ride, I'll get him. If anything, and I mean anything, seems strange, call Luca or me. Remember this above everything else: if Mrs. Washington uses the word *fiddlesticks*, that means hell is about to hit. Get yourself and your aunt to a safe place. Start scoping out where that safe place should be and let us know. Did you get all that?"

"Yeah, I got it. Fiddlesticks."

When they entered the hospital, they were told Nelson was awake and able to take visitors. Eric nearly ran to the room. When he entered, Luca sat in a chair near the bed where Nelson was propped up on pillows wearing a sling on his right arm. "Man, I'm glad to see you. How are you doing?"

Nelson lifted a distinguished brow. "I'm not sure, Master Eric. Why don't you tell me? After all, you're the one who can predict the future."

"What are you talking about?"

"*This is going to be a great day. I can feel it in my bones.* Do you remember saying that yesterday…sir?"

Chapter Twenty-Nine

Saturday, September 22—Life of the Party

Joy was at the table, sipping her coffee, when Eric came into the kitchen closely followed by Mugsy. How did kids and dogs have so much energy in the morning? She wished she could stay in bed all day. "Did Mugsy have any problem sleeping in a new place last night?"

"Are you kidding?" Eric laughed. "To Mugsy, home is his fluffy blue bed. Wherever big blue goes, he goes." Mugsy yapped in agreement.

Eric bent over the stove and then gave her a frown. "Hey! This is Saturday. We usually have something cool for breakfast on Saturday…like pancakes."

Mrs. Washington tapped the drips off her wooden spoon and laid it aside. "Listen here, little mister." She only called him that when she was annoyed. "I happen to know you'll be eating all the junk food you can hold later at your party. This morning, you'll have a healthy breakfast. There's not a thing wrong with eggs and grits. I even put in a little cheddar cheese, the way your uncle likes them."

Eric brightened. "He does?"

Joy watched Eric dig into his food without another complaint.

It had been quiet around the house last night

without Luca. Had he finally left the hospital and gotten a good night's sleep? Why should she care?

It was strange sleeping in her own bed again. She'd changed the sheets as soon as she got home, but her pillows still smelled like his stupid cologne. Maybe she should throw them into the washing machine. Mrs. Washington refilled her cup without a word. "I appreciate all your help, but I hope you don't feel like you have to take care of us."

The older woman buttered her toast with vigor. "Don't give it another thought, Miss Sullivan. I'm going to enjoy my little vacation and let the men find out what it's like not having someone to follow them around picking up their messes. At least one person here doesn't complain about every decision I make."

"Sorry, Mrs. Washington," Eric grumbled.

She reached over to pat his shoulder. "You are forgiven *only* because you gave up that cozy bed of yours and slept on the sofa. That was very gentlemanly of you."

Luca's staff were good for Eric. They kept him in line without being harsh. Joy was glad to have their help. "You always have a place here with us." She told the runaway cook. "I know it can't be easy being the only woman in a house full of men."

Mrs. Washington chucked. "With Nelson in the hospital and me here, a couple of those men will find out it's not so easy to run a large household."

That made Joy's mind lean in another direction. "I just hope I can keep this small household going until I can find a job."

Mrs. Washington turned to speak directly. "You don't need a job, honey. All you need are a few new supplies. You have to have inspections and permits to open a shop, but all you need is your license to do hair. If your clients can't come to you, then you can simply go to them. Start calling your clients. I bet you'll have plenty of people agree."

Joy thought of the client list she kept on her laptop computer. Thankfully she'd brought it in the house the day of the fire and hadn't left it in the shop like she sometimes did. "That could be enough to keep me afloat until something comes open."

Eric gave them both a worried look. "Do you think my party will come off okay? I mean since you both bailed on Uncle Luca."

Mrs. Washington looked offended. "Would I leave something as important as your birthday party to chance? I had everything in order by the middle of the week."

Eric turned pleading eyes to Joy. "Arnold said he's bringing Bryce and his mom to the party. Would you mind if we gave Janet a ride? Her dad has to work today, and her mom has to visit her grandma at some old folks' home."

Joy felt a sudden surge of panic. She wasn't ready to face Luca again so soon. "Isn't your uncle sending someone to pick you up?"

Eric added a spoon of jelly to his toast. "No. He asked if he should, but I told him you guys wouldn't ditch my first birthday party since…well, you know."

Mrs. Washington said, as she squeezed Joy's hand and winked, "Of course, we wouldn't. We were just talking about it and thought you wouldn't want to show up with us old folks."

Joy was incredibly grateful for Mrs. Washington's

quick thinking. It was days like today when Eric would miss his parents the most. She had to be adult enough to deal with this.

Eric grinned. "Are you kidding? I'll be the only guy showing up with three women."

So, it was decided.

When they arrived, Luca's back patio looked like a carnival with music, balloons, games, and food. Striped tents had been erected at each end of the pool, one marked *boys*, and the other *girls*. Joy had never seen anything like it. Luca had gone all out. And speaking of the devil, he was walking her way. She looked around and realized she was standing alone.

"I love that dress." Luca smiled as his eyes traveled to her feet and back. "You were wearing it the first time I kissed you."

That was on her mind when she'd chosen to wear it. "Was I? I don't recall."

He held out his hand. "Can I get a few minutes with you in my study? There's something I'd like to discuss with you privately."

Although she longed to, Joy didn't reach for him. "I don't know if that's a good idea."

Luca laughed and dropped his hands into his pockets. "It's about the custody case. I promise no monkey business."

When he sat on the sofa, she chose a chair at the other end. He smiled and slid closer. "I've seen the document that man in prison wrote regarding your mother. It was atrocious. I had a friend of a friend look into him for me."

Joy let her eyes wander around the room. "I don't care what he wrote. I don't even care if he is my father.

It shouldn't be pertinent to the case."

"You're right, but I thought you'd want to know, this guy is getting paid. A hundred dollars is going into his account at the prison every week. It started the day he signed that letter. I can't let my brother and his shyster lawyer get away with this. The state has his DNA on file. I'd like to get a sample of yours."

She gazed at her lap. "You want to see if our DNA matches?"

"No," Luca insisted. "I want to prove the man is lying and that my brother put him up to it."

Finally, she looked straight into Luca's eyes. "You're having Eric's DNA tested, too, aren't you?"

Luca nodded. "It's the best way I can think of to pull the rug out from under Daniel's feet. If Eric isn't his grandson, he can't be the boy's next of kin."

"Are you trying to find out who his real father is?"

"No." Luca looked appalled. "I don't want to know. If I did, I'd feel duty bound to tell the man he had a son. He'd have every right to take him away from us. We can't risk that."

Joy noticed he was saying *us* and *we*, as though they were still partnering in this endeavor. Were they? She had to know. "If Daniel isn't Eric's next of kin, who is?"

Luca took her hand. "Only you, Joy. You would most likely be awarded sole guardianship. I hope you'd still let me be in his life. I truly do love that kid."

"Okay." Joy was satisfied with his response. "I'll consider taking the DNA test. I'll let you know on Monday."

Joy started to leave, but Luca called out to her. "I'm not ready to give up on you either. I want to be part of your life as well."

How big of a part, was what Joy wished she could ask but didn't dare.

****

Eric sat in the back seat of the car with Janet while Joy drove them and Mrs. Washington back to Summer Springs. It had been an awesome party. Now, Janet was letting him hold her hand. No one would know in the dark, but he'd never forget. This was the start of something big.

They pulled into the driveway, and the headlights swept over the house. He thought he saw movement by the back gate.

Mrs. Washington pulled a gun from her purse. For the first time since he'd met her, she looked like a soldier straight off the pages of Uncle Luca's books. "Everyone, stay in the car. Someone is in the backyard. Call Luca. If you hear a shot, get out of here. Go to the laundromat. We'll meet there."

She ran from the car and through the gate.

He couldn't believe what he'd seen until Janet squeezed his hand. "Mrs. Washington carries a gun? I never knew she had a gun in that ugly old bag."

Janet grabbed his sleeve with her free hand. "It's a German-made automatic, like the one my dad has." Her knowledge of firearms boosted her a little higher in his affections.

Seconds later, as Joy spoke to Luca, Mrs. Washington returned. "Put him on speaker phone. He may as well hear this, too." Mrs. Washington continued speaking while everyone listened in silence. "It was a teenage boy, older than Eric, maybe seventeen or eighteen. He said he was just cutting through the yard. I couldn't detain him. I don't think we should take any chances. We should have the cops sweep the place for explosives, listening devices, and cameras—make sure the little bastard wasn't working for the enemy."

"I agree," Eric heard his uncle say. "I'm on my way. Call Detective Anderson."

When the police arrived, everyone left the car but him and Janet, who were told to wait.

Janet watched the action with wide eyes. "It sure isn't boring around your family."

Eric was glad she couldn't see how red his face was under all the flashing lights. "Just part of the entertainment we provide."

She scooted a little closer. "I hope you liked the T-shirt I got you. It's hard to buy for a boy who already has everything."

It wouldn't matter if she'd given him a stick of gum. He'd treasure it. "It's great. I love monster trucks. I'm going to wear it to school on Monday."

She scooted a tiny bit closer, again. "There is something else I'd like to give you," she said shyly.

Eric watched the area of the seat between them get smaller. "You don't have to give me anything."

Janet giggled. "I was going to ask if I could kiss you, silly."

"Kiss…me…I'd like that."

It wasn't just one kiss. And it wasn't just a baby kiss. It was the most fantastic thing that had ever happened in his entire life. Then someone tapped on the window. He looked around Janet to stare straight at Luca.

"You can walk your girlfriend home now."

Janet grabbed her phone and checked the screen.

"My curfew is ten o'clock. We'd better hurry."

By the time they'd reached her door, Eric had worked up the nerve to ask, "Do you think you'd like to, you know, be my girlfriend?"

"I already am." Janet laughed before kissing him one last time. "Your uncle just said so."

Chapter Thirty

Sunday, September 23—Information Overload

"I want to go home."

Luca stood beside Nelson's hospital bed. "I wish you could. I could use another set of eyes on the current situation. But I feel like you aren't ready. Your shoulder is still in bad shape. We can't be positive that bullet wasn't intended for you. You're safe here until this blows over or you're in better fighting form."

The older man sneered. "You haven't asked me why I came to the courthouse looking for you."

"I knew you were going to say Eric's DNA didn't match David's."

"Don't you want to know who his father is?"

"No! I didn't ask you to look for that information. I don't care who it is. Don't you dare tell me."

"You need to know, Luca."

Nelson rarely called him by his first name. It only happened when he went into father mode and wanted to say something for Luca's own good. This wouldn't do him good at all. He changed the subject. "Eric's party was a tremendous success."

"As most are, I imagine." Nelson pouted.

"I caught him making out with Janet in the back seat of Joy's car."

Nelson quirked a brow and nodded. "Our little boy is growing up."

"Arnold showed up to the party with his new girlfriend, also."

Nelson crossed his arms. The new subject was starting to interest him. "Do tell."

"She's a pleasant-looking little blond woman. Dinah Foster, as you suspected. I like her."

"Ah, the world moves on while I sit in this bed and rot." Luca laughed until Nelson asked, "And, how is your love life?"

Luca frowned and turned toward the window. "I prefer to think of it as temporarily stalled and not blown out of the water."

"I don't understand." Nelson struggled to sit straighter against the raised back of his bed. "You're a young man with looks, charm, and class. You've never been involved in a serious relationship. And yet, your brother has the looks, manners, and personality of a walrus. He's been to the altar five times. What is his secret?"

"I don't know…drugs, alcohol, blackmail perhaps."

"You need a family, sir. I've decided having Master Eric around the house isn't nearly as horrible as I'd feared. But I'd like to start at the beginning with the next child."

"Now you sound like my mother."

Nelson closed his eyes with a blissful smile. "Mmm, just the mention of the woman brings wonderful music to my mind. I'll surely have a sweet dream tonight."

"I don't need to know that," Luca groaned. "I'm

leaving."

"More time to dream."

Just as Luca reached for the door handle, Nelson stopped the world. "Luca, he's your son. Eric is yours. I can't keep that information from you."

Luca stood in stunned silence for several seconds, then returned to Nelson's bedside. "Are you sure there's no mistake?"

"I'm positive."

"I don't want you to tell a single soul. Not anyone...not ever. Do you understand? Swear to me you won't tell."

"The boy has a right to know."

"I'll decide if and when I'll impart that information."

****

Luca sat in his car, forehead against the steering wheel, thoughts shooting around like marbles in a pinball machine. Would Eric resent him? Would Joy hate him? Would he be a good dad? What would David say if he were here? Could Eric handle this at his age? Did Melissa know? Why had David chosen him to raise Eric? Would Joy think he was trying to trick her? Would Eric feel betrayed? Could his brother use this against him?

Light suddenly made everything brighter. A cloud had moved from over the sun. He was a dad. Eric was his son. He wanted to shout with pride, but at least for now, no one could know. He might never be in a position to say it out loud, but he'd hold it tightly in his heart.

****

Joy stood at the kitchen sink, bathing Mugsy. They

were actually finished, but Mugsy loved baths more than any dog she'd ever seen. He sat preening while she sprayed his back.

She pictured her bank register in her mind. Luca had paid her five hundred dollars per week in the time he'd stayed at her home. Most of that had been saved. She had enough to last for as much as two months if she was careful.

Suddenly, Mugsy began yapping and took two quick laps around the sink. He jumped to the counter top and shook water everywhere. He then leaped through the air into Eric's outstretched arms. "Whose dog is this?" she playfully teased.

"What can I say? We've bonded. I fill the bowls, and he empties them. He poops, and I pick it up. It's a system that works for us."

"I suppose you're looking for food."

"I wouldn't turn down some leftover chicken and potato salad. Life is perfect with two of the best cooks in Florida at my fingertips."

Joy laughed and dried herself with the towel she'd intended for the dog.

Eric turned serious. "I kind of wanted to talk to you while Mrs. Washington was outside weeding the flowers."

"Okay. What's on your mind?"

"Do you think my parents were ever in love, or did they just get married because she was pregnant?"

Joy brought the food containers to the table and handed Eric a fork. "I think your dad wouldn't have made that commitment if he hadn't had a deep feeling for your mom. Lots of guys would just take off. They seemed to love each other in the beginning, but they were awfully young. Maybe they mistook that for actually being in love. There is a difference."

Eric spoke around a mouthful of chicken. "What's the difference?"

"I think you can love a lot of people, but being in love is only for that special someone." She sat across from him. "They're the one who matters more than yourself. Nothing can change that. Some people lose the person they're in love with and are lucky enough to fall in love a second time, but not always."

"Why do you think they stopped loving each other?"

"I guess, when they realized it wasn't the in-love kind of love, they were disappointed. Their expectations hadn't been met. They thought they'd lost their chance for the real thing. Neither of them wanted to be the one to give in and call it quits. The resentments kept building, and they started doing things to hurt each other. They each probably hoped the other would walk away."

"You mean like Dad running off to sleep with hookers and Mom getting drunk in her room? But it felt like they were both hurting me just as much."

Joy brought a glass of milk to the table. "They didn't see that, Eric. They were both blinded by self-pity. That's a very destructive thing."

Eric watched her with a sincere expression. "Who do you love?"

"Lots of people I guess…but mostly you."

"Have you ever been in love?"

An image of Luca popped into her mind, but she shook it away. "Not yet."

"When do you know you're in love?"

"It doesn't happen until your mind has fully matured. You still have a while before it happens. Until then, you'll find people you simply love."

"You mean, like the way mom loved other guys before they got married?"

Joy thought this conversation had started because of his feelings for Janet, but now she suspected their meeting at the courthouse may have had some influence.

"Eric, sometimes people look for a way to make themselves feel better when something bad has happened. Take for instance, when your mom was abandoned by her father. But those things can hurt them worse. Some people turn to alcohol, drugs, cutting, or sex with lots of people."

Eric got up to pour another glass of milk. Joy could almost feel his mind working. "Aunt Joy, when do you think is a good time for people to start having sex?"

She hadn't seen that coming. "I'm not very experienced in this field. When it comes to boys anyway. Maybe you should save that question for your Uncle Luca."

Saved by the bell—or the ringing of her phone.

"Janet isn't here. We haven't seen her since Eric walked her home last night," Joy said into the phone. Trying not to look overly concerned Joy turned to Eric. "Honey, have you heard from Janet today?"

"She called this morning. She said she was going to go for a run, then shower and go shopping with her mom. I've been waiting for her to get back."

"Her mom says she hasn't seen her since breakfast. Would you mind calling her friends and see if you can find her?"

Eric dropped his fork and looked like he was going to be sick. "Okay. I'll get started right now."

Chapter Thirty-One

Monday, September 24—The Takedown (Part One)

Luca watched the smaller window on the left end of the house through binoculars. He could see Eric washing dishes. He was a good kid. Joy was good for him. He was a lot more responsible than he had been a few weeks ago. Actually, he was more responsible than Luca himself at that age.

He could see the worry in his son's eyes. Janet was his first girlfriend. Probably his first kiss. She'd been missing now for almost thirty-six hours. Was that a coincidence? How much bad luck could a family have? If it was the same person who set the fire, took the shot, and all the rest—why Janet? Eric could be the only reason. Perhaps it was a way to lure the boy to a place or an action. It didn't make much sense.

A rumble of thunder followed seconds later by lightning announced the onset of rain. Dammit, he wouldn't be able to see much longer. He was glad the garbage cans were under cover of the new carport. That would be Eric's final job for the night.

At that moment, movement from the left caught his eye. A large figure in dark clothing slowly crept along the fence staying low to blend with the bushes. If he called the house, the sound might scare the person away. No, he wanted to know who was there.

Quickly slipping on a lightweight poncho and boonie hat left over from his days in the service, Luca stealthily made his way out of the empty house. He crossed the street two lots away from where the overhead light had been disabled. That allowed him to approach Joy's house from the opposite side and sneak around the back.

Light from the kitchen illuminated Eric until the door closed. All went dark again. The man sprang onto the boy at that precise moment. He didn't have a chance to make a sound before a hand covered his mouth and a gun was at his head.

A roar louder than Luca had ever heard before sounded inside his head. He could feel the blood pumping through his veins. There was no rest between his heartbeats. This was an enemy like he'd never faced before. This man was threatening one of the two things he treasured most in his life. He had one chance to save Eric before the man could take his shot. He had to make it count.

Luca moved through the softest soil without a sound as he slid a hunting knife from its leather sheath. He grabbed the man's gun with his left hand, raising it skyward to slice through the tendons in his wrist. A blast sounded from the weapon. The man screamed. Eric dodged to the side.

"Fiddlesticks, fiddlesticks," Eric yelled.

Mrs. Washington flew out the door, but before either of the adults could react, Eric was on top the man, beating his face and head. "Where is she? What have you done to her?" he yelled.

The man cowered on the ground with his arms

raised to cover his face. "What are you talking about? Stop! Someone help me!"

Oh God, with only those few words Luca recognized the voice. He reached down and pulled the black knit cap off the man's head. Daniel.

In the next minute, Joy was holding on to Eric to prevent him from doing further damage to his grandfather while Mrs. Washington pinned Daniel Wolff to the ground.

Luca spoke to the nine-one-one operator. "Please see they send an ambulance. And make sure Detective Anderson gets the message." He could already hear sirens approaching.

"You can't do this to me." Daniel insisted. "I'll see all of you in jail before the night's over. I could be bleeding to death. I can't move my hand."

Luca knelt by his head. "You know how every time I do something you don't like, you ask if I learned it in the marines? Well, this time, the answer is yes. If you don't shut up, I can cut your tongue out just as quickly."

"You threatened me. Everyone here heard you."

Mrs. Washington grabbed his collar. "I didn't hear a sound."

"Get off me, you cow."

She gave him a swift elbow to his kidney. "That kind of talk isn't advisable, Mr. Wolff."

Daniel stayed quiet until he was handcuffed to a gurney in the ambulance. "These other people are the ones you should be arresting. Three of them have assaulted me." His swollen, purple nose still bled from Eric's beating. "I only came here to see my grandson and look what he did to me. He's been in trouble before, you know."

Detective Anderson walked to the door of the ambulance. "What about this, Mr. Wolff?" he held up a clear plastic evidence bag which held a .38 caliber handgun.

"My brother is a violent man. I knew I might have to defend myself."

Anderson nudged the officer who'd be escorting Daniel to the hospital. "Make sure you read him his rights."

Daniel ranted as the doors of the ambulance closed. "I want to call my lawyer. I'll go over your head. You know the police chief is a good friend of my father."

"I can't believe this," Luca mumbled.

"Nothing surprises me anymore," Anderson replied. "People do strange things for strange reasons. I could tell you some wild stories. You could write a whole new series of books."

Luca asked, "Do you think he has anything to do with the girl who disappeared from next door yesterday?"

"No. We've already checked his alibi for that time. He was at the club." Anderson used a regal tone on the last couple words and rolled his eyes.

"You questioned him?"

Anderson nodded. "I've had a funny feeling about him for a while." He held up the evidence bag again. "At least now we have something for ballistics to compare with the bullet we got from your man, Nelson. I'm taking this to the lab right now."

When Luca turned toward the house, Joy was standing in the doorway.

She walked down the steps with her arms folded. "I

guess you're pretty pumped up—coming to our rescue like that. You were watching the house again. You really do believe I'm not capable of taking care of Eric." She stepped closer. "Something like this could happen to anyone at any time. I'm not a damsel in distress waiting for a prince to rescue me. You can't always be around to charge in and save us."

He closed the gap between them. "I could be if you'd let me."

"You hide too many secrets, Luca." She put her hands against his chest and pushed him back. "I don't know if I can trust you."

"Trust is earned, but I don't feel like you've given me a fair chance to prove myself. You jump to assumptions…like thinking I don't believe you're capable. I know you are. I believe you are smarter, stronger, and more competent then you think."

She turned her eyes to the ground and didn't reply.

Luca walked past her to say goodbye to Eric. "You know, a simple thank-you would have been sufficient." It stung when she said he kept too many secrets because there was another bigger one he was still holding from her.

****

Eric heard Luca's footsteps coming down the hall. He wiped his face on the tail of his T-shirt. His life sucked enough right now without somebody catching him crying like a baby.

Luca sat on the edge of the bed beside him. "You okay, buddy?"

"I guess I'm sorry for plowing into Grand-Dan like that."

Luca laughed. "I'm not. I thought it was pretty

freaking awesome."

"It didn't do any good, though. I don't think he's the one who took Janet. I don't know what to do now. My chest hurts all the time since she's been gone. I feel like I'm going to have a heart attack."

Luca ruffled his hair. "It's not a heart attack, Eric, its anxiety. I'd be more surprised if you didn't feel the way you do. You care about Janet. Try to remember, everybody in Summer Springs is looking for her. No stone will be left unturned."

"I keep thinking she may be hurt somewhere—maybe out in the rain, cold, and hungry. She was only wearing a tank top and shorts when she left the house."

"I can't tell you not to worry, Eric." Luca brushed the hair from his forehead. "Just don't give up hope."

Eric nodded. The lump in his throat was too big to let him speak.

"Are you and your aunt Joy doing okay together?"

"I guess," he shrugged. "She's cool. We even talked about love and stuff the other day."

His uncle's eyes widened. "Is that right? How did it go?"

"She knew all about the love stuff, but when I brought up sex, she said you had more experience in that department."

"Oh...okay...what did you want to know?"

"I asked her when's a good time for people to start having sex."

"It'll be a few years before you have to worry about that, but you have to give it serious consideration all your life. Every time you're with a girl."

This might be harder than Eric had thought. "Every single time?"

"Well, let's say every time you're with someone new."

"Why? Once you've done it once it seems like it would be fairly easy."

"Listen to me, Eric." Luca put on his serious face and thought for a minute. "Any time you're with a girl, you leave a mark on her soul. You have to ask yourself if you care. If you don't care, you should walk away. It's not right, simple as that. If you do care, you have to ask yourself another question. Will the mark you leave be a pleasant memory for her or one she'll come to regret later on—because she'll carry that mark on her soul for the rest of her life."

"It sounds more complicated than I thought."

"Yes, it is." Luca kissed the top of his head and stood to leave. "You'll find out that most of the best things are."

This was something he'd have to discuss with Doctor Johnson.

Chapter Thirty-Two

Tuesday, September 25—The Takedown (Part Two)

Joy was putting away the groceries she and Mrs. Washington had just carried in from the car. She felt weak from lack of sleep. The clock on the stove read three fifteen. "It's almost time for Eric to get home from school. I hope it went okay. He probably didn't get any more rest last night than I did."

Mrs. Washington sat down at the table. "I can't believe I slept until after he'd left this morning. I haven't even looked at the newspaper that came this morning. I wonder if they mention what happened here last night."

Joy laughed. "Won't the elder Mr. Wolff be proud of that?"

"Oh, look." The older woman held up the front page. "They have a picture of the football team from Eric's school."

"It's that time of year already?"

Mrs. Washington pointed at a face on the top row of the picture. "Look at this. That's the boy who cut through the yard the other night after Eric's party. I wonder if he knows him."

Joy slid into the chair at the other side of the table.

"I'm a little worried about Eric. He's so concerned about Janet, I wouldn't doubt that his school work is suffering."

Mrs. Washington was very quiet and still for a moment. Joy wondered if she was praying. "Miss Sullivan, I want to tell you something. It's something I've never told anyone but Mr. Washington since the day it happened."

"What is it?" Joy asked.

After a deep breath, the housekeeper continued. "When I was a young girl, I lived pretty far from town. My father was a farmer, and my mother ran off when I was ten. I was a hard worker but horribly naïve. I'd get off the school bus on the road nearest our house and walk about a quarter mile passing a train track. Often times old railroad cars would be left on the side rails there." She stopped for a moment and sighed. "One day, just before my seventeenth birthday, a man was hiding in one of those cars."

Joy grabbed her hand. "Oh no, Mrs. Washington, you don't have to tell me. It must be so hard for you."

"No, I have to get it off my chest." She sighed again. "My daddy drove me back and forth after that, but we didn't talk about it. I even quit talking to my friends. I felt so dirty. That's when I stopped being Ginger. A year later I was Private Truman. That was my maiden name. The only man in my life afterward was my sweet Mr. Washington. He was so kind, gentle, and understanding. The only thing that devastated me more was the day I learned of my husband's death. I just can't stop thinking about what may be happening to that poor little girl. The longer she's gone, the more it bothers me."

"I guess it must." Joy hugged her companion. "If she gets home safely, we'll make sure to help with whatever she needs and not let her lose who she is."

Mrs. Washington went to her room for a nap before Arnold dropped Eric off on his way to the Foster house. Joy hadn't moved from the table, deep in thought.

"Hey, Aunt Joy, is everything okay?"

"Yeah, sure." The newspaper still lay open on the table. "Eric, do you know this boy on the football team?"

Eric squinted at the place Joy's finger was pointing. "Oh, that guy is a major butthead. His name is Mitch Frazier. For some reason, he really has it in for me. He's been kind of quiet for the last couple days. Probably because of Janet. She went out with him briefly at the beginning of school. When she saw how he treated people, she dumped him, though."

Joy watched for Eric's reaction. "Mrs. Washington says he's the boy who went through the yard Saturday night, but I've never seen him. Does he live close by?"

"No way." Eric looked confused. "His folks own that orange grove outside the south end of town. He works at the Burger Hut after school and drives a beat-up old station wagon. Why would he be walking through our yard?"

She looked back at the picture. "Good question."

Joy couldn't get it out of her mind for the next two hours. Finally, she decided to wake up Mrs. Washington. "Get your boots on, Ginger. We're going on a recon mission."

Mrs. Washington threw off the covers. "Now you're speaking my language."

It was three and a half hours and a bag of burgers

later when the three of them watched Mitch walk to his rusty brown vehicle. They stayed a fair distance behind him as they followed him home. When he turned onto a side road into the grove instead of going down the driveway to his house, they decided they'd have to leave the car between some trees and try to trail him on foot. The mud from irrigation water made his tire tracks easy to see, but the sun was going down.

Mrs. Washington gave instructions in a whisper. "Turn the ringers off on your phones, people. We don't want to give away our location."

Joy suddenly wondered if they should have brought some kind of weapons. But this was a high school kid, even if he was twice her size.

They stopped a few yards back when they found him walking up to a huge, square, yellow container. It looked like one of the trash dumpsters you'd see at a construction site. He threw two bottles of water and a full Burger Hut bag into the bin.

"Hey," Janet yelled from inside the bin. "When are you going to get me out of here?"

Mrs. Washington had to grab Eric and put her hand over his mouth. "Stay quiet," she whispered. "Let's see what's going on."

Mitch yelled back to Janet, "It's your own damned fault. You shouldn't have run off and jumped into that thing. You shouldn't have broken up with me in the first place. Everything would have been fine if that brat, Eric, hadn't shown up. You think he's so great—well, where is he now?"

They heard Janet's voice again. "Eric is better than you'll ever be, you Neanderthal. Give me back my phone, so I can at least let my parents know where I am.

They can send someone to help me get out of this thing."

"If I did that. I'd get in trouble for taking you."

"So, what are you going to do? You can't keep me in here forever."

Mitch started walking back to his car. "I know. I'll figure something out."

When his car was a safe distance away, Eric broke free and ran to the bin. He scaled up the side and vaulted over it, probably the same way Janet had two days earlier. Joy was already calling the emergency services.

Mrs. Washington grinned proudly. "We do good work, Joy."

****

Luca found Joy sitting in the lobby at the police station. "Who's the hero now?"

She hid a smile before looking up. "It was a team effort."

"You'll never admit how awesome you are, but that's one of the things I love about you, Sullivan."

She narrowed her eyes. "How did you find out what happened?"

"I got a call from the desk sergeant. You'll never guess what they found under a tarp in one of the barns when they were looking for the Frazier kid."

"No," she said with huge eyes. "Your car?"

"Yep, now they have him on grand theft and kidnapping. There may be a few more charges after Janet finishes her statement. The poor kid could have been bitten by a snake or raccoon in that trailer."

"She should see a doctor. It rained several times when she was trapped in that thing."

Luca sat down beside her. "Always wanting to take care of people, there's another great quality you have. I'd really like to kiss you right now."

"What about keeping a respectable distance until Eric is sorted out?"

He lifted a brow. "Umm, great memory, too."

"I'm glad you're both here," Detective Anderson said as he entered. "I have something I want to show you guys."

He sat the two of them at a table in a private room and opened a laptop computer. After bringing up Daniel's interrogation tape, he fast forwarded through the first half. "Nothing there but a lot of whining and threats," he remarked. "But wait for it." When the video slowed to average speed, they saw the detectives leave the room. Gerald Wolff came in shortly after.

"What the hell is going on, Daniel? Why would you do such a thing? You had a gun to your own grandson's head."

Daniel tried to turn away, but there was no way to avoid the old man in the cramped room.

"Did you blow up Luca's house?"

"They can't prove anything." Daniel blurted. *"I'm paying the guy a fortune to keep his mouth shut. The idiot broke parole and got himself sent back to prison."*

Gerald hit the table top with his opened hand. *"Is this the same man who wrote the letter about the Sullivan woman? I thought that was on the level."*

"You don't know everything, Father. This whole mess is your fault."

The old man harrumphed. *"I refuse to believe that. I've never done anything to you."*

Daniel whined, *"You've never trusted me. You've*

never believed in me. You treat me like a child."

"You act like a child. You wouldn't be penniless and have to live off me if you'd made good decisions. Five ex-wives, Daniel? Then those stupid investments."

"I was trying to live up to your standards, Father. It's just not possible."

"What does that have to do with Luca?"

Daniel tried to raise his hands, but they were chained to the floor. *"He was a mistake from the beginning. You should never have had him. He hasn't shown you the respect I have. He doesn't deserve to inherit from you."*

Gerald looked shocked. *"Is that what this is about, Daniel? You want my money?"*

"I have to have it. I need it." Daniel sounded desperate. *"You can't live much longer, then what's going to happen to me?"*

"You were the one who set fire to Miss Sullivan's beauty salon."

"I wanted to get her out of the way. Her and Luca and the brat got all of David and Melissa's money. I need that money. They shouldn't have been in your will, either. It was up to me to determine what they'd inherit."

"You killed them. My God. You killed your own son."

Daniel began to cry. *"He was coming between us. You respected him more than you did me. Michael Knight told me about your will. That was the last straw."*

"I hope they put you away for the rest of your life. You are no longer my son."

"Knight will get me out of this. He's a smart

lawyer."

"*No, he won't,*" Gerald declared. "*Not after I testify against you.*"

"*You can't do that, Father!*"

"*Don't call me that,*" Gerald yelled. "*I realize now that I only had one son who grew up to be a man and it wasn't you. The only thing I regret is the way I've treated him.*"

The door slammed as Gerald left Daniel a quivering mess.

Anderson threw his fist in the air. "We've got him dead to rights."

"I guess you do." Luca felt numb. "You implied earlier that you'd suspected Daniel. What tipped you off?"

"First of all, he was the only person to touch that plane before your nephew and his wife took off for Mexico. He was the one who'd suggested the trip. After a little investigating, we found out he'd been in phone contact with the convict he mentioned on the day your house was blown up. After your meeting at the courthouse, he was the first one of you out the door. That shot came from the parking lot where he'd gone to his car. Were you aware that he belongs to a gun club? I'm a little surprised he missed his target. Another thing I wanted to tell you is, I'm sorry he slipped away from us and got to Eric."

"I'm not." Luca laughed. "The kid is tough, and we were there to back him up. Daniel is finally behind bars where he belongs."

Chapter Thirty-Three

Monday, October 8—A Healing

It was eight in the morning when Joy heard a knock on her door. Even though she knew Daniel was in jail, the past few weeks had made her nervous. Joy had lived alone for three years, and now Eric was with her, but she still jumped at every unexpected sound. Joy tiptoed to the window and peeked through the blinds. Luca stood on her doorstep.

"What do you want?" she asked in a whisper when she opened the door.

He laughed. "Good morning to you, too."

"Shhh, Eric is sleeping in. He doesn't have school today."

"I know. Columbus Day," he whispered. "Do you have coffee?"

She waved him inside and led him to the kitchen. Being further from Eric's room, she could speak normally. "Did you just come over for coffee? I happen to know you have an abundant supply at your house." She poured two cups from the full pot.

"I came to see if Eric wanted to hang out today. I know Janet is out of town with her family, so I thought we could shoot some hoops, catch a movie, and grab a pizza, or whatever."

255

"You have such a way with words, Mister Author."

His smile dazzled her. "Thanks."

She sat at the table knowing he'd follow. "He was at your house all weekend. Why didn't you just keep him there?"

"I don't have to work. My new manuscript got the final approval from the publisher. They sent me word last night. I don't feel like starting on a new project until after our court date. It's too hard to concentrate."

"Now that your brother has been arrested, I don't think there'll be any more surprises. What are you worried about?"

His smile faded into a mask of misery. "I miss you."

"We shouldn't be having this conversation."

"We'll have to talk about it sooner or later. I don't plan to give up. We're good together. We're both good for Eric."

She'd have to be adult about this. "You're the one who said we should cool things off until everything was sorted out. After all that's happened, I believe you were right. One of us is going to leave the courthouse next week very disappointed. It may take time to get past that."

"I wish it were over with now." Luca declared. "I know Eric will be okay, no matter which way the judge rules. I just want to make sure we're okay, too."

"What do you have to be worried about?" Joy's phone, between them on the table, rang. The display across the front read *Dr. Johnson*.

"That's one thing to worry about right there."

"Don't be ridiculous." Joy answered the call putting it on speaker phone. "Hello, Dr. Johnson. Luca and I are both here. What can we do for you?"

"I'm glad to have you both on the line. I wanted to talk to you about Eric."

"I didn't think you were allowed to discuss Eric with us," Luca said.

"I can't tell you what's been said in our sessions, but I can talk to you about something that's bothering me about him."

Joy looked at Luca, worried as she responded. "That sounds serious. I thought he was doing well."

"Basically, he is. He feels much more secure, thanks to the two of you. And, his confidence has soared. I think we can give part of the credit for that to his new girlfriend. There's just one issue he's having a hard time with."

"What's that?" Luca asked.

"His mother. You've both talked to him about the reasons that may have led to her unhappiness and subsequent alcohol problem. At the same time, he's been learning about integrity, responsibility, and honor. I believe he feels like he failed her, he didn't protect her the way he should have. Now, it's too late."

"What can we do about it now that she's gone?" Joy asked.

"Eric knows her father was at the root of her problems, and I agree. I know there isn't a relationship between them, but is there any way he could speak to his maternal grandfather?"

"What good would that do?" Luca asked. "The boy would probably take one look at the old man and go off like a roman candle."

"I know. I think that would be the best thing for him. Give him a chance to be his mother's champion.

You have to admit, the guy's got it coming."

Joy was genuinely shocked. "I can't believe you'd let him do that."

"I can make it happen," Luca replied.

After she'd closed her phone, Joy turned to Luca. "We don't even know where Mr. Sullivan is."

"I know exactly where he is. I google everyone. Google is my best friend." He punched a couple numbers on his own phone and said, "Nelson, get the phone number for Donald L. Sullivan at Midtown Condominiums in St. Augustine. Tell him I want a meeting with him this afternoon."

Just as Luca settled into his car, his phone rang. It was Dr. Johnson again. "I guess you and Joy are an item again. I was surprised to hear you were there, this early in the morning."

He had the good doctor on the run. "I'm working on it. I think I have a good shot."

"Let's not pretend here. You know I'm interested too. I don't poach on another man's territory, but have no doubt, I will move in if you don't make this work."

Luca laughed. "You'd better look elsewhere, Doc. I always win."

****

His uncle Luca had been right. When you look good, you feel great. Eric practically strutted in black slacks and boots with a gold silk dress shirt. His hair was styled on top and off the face, the way his aunt Joy liked it. He knew he was walking into a lion's den, and he intended to look like the alpha, small but mighty.

There'd been a day when something like this would cause him to curl into a quivering ball, but now he felt lava in his veins. He hoped Aunt Joy was right about loved ones watching over you. He intended to make his parents proud.

Luca looked damned sharp too, wearing a tan suit with a caramel colored T-shirt. He'd said he was coming along to get them through the door and act as backup. His aunt Joy had to stay home because this guy hated her. That was another thing Eric hated about him.

The man who opened the door was the one they'd come to see. Eric recognized him immediately from an old picture his mother kept on her dresser. He was older, heavier, and had gray hair sprinkled through the red. At a closer view, Eric could see his grandfather had the same blue eyes as his mother. He was showing his confidence by going casual in knee-length navy-blue shorts and a striped polo shirt. This was his turf. He didn't need to prove himself. That was fine.

The man reached past Eric to shake Luca's hand. "Come in, come in," he said as he led them to his study. "I'm quite curious as to why you asked for this meeting, Mr. Wolff. I have to ask though, do you always bring your kid along? Have a seat."

Luca sat in a high-backed leather chair. Eric stood beside him. "Actually, Mr. Sullivan, your meeting is with him. I'm just along for the ride." He looked at Eric. "Tell him who you are, kid."

Eric held a steady hand out to the man. "My name is Eric Wolff. I'm your grandson."

Sullivan turned to Luca. "Is this some kind of a joke?"

Eric refused to be ignored. "Not at all, sir. My mother is Melissa Sullivan-Wolff, your daughter."

"I suppose you're here to hit me up for money," Sullivan sneered. "Did your grandmother put you up to this scheme? I gave her a fair settlement when I left."

"Well, sir, whether that settlement was fair is debatable," Eric stated. "But I have no need for your money. I have sizable assets of my own. You might even say—I could buy you three times over. I'm here to talk to you about what you did to my mother."

Sullivan looked to Luca. "I guess my daughter is married to you. She didn't do too badly for herself."

Luca shook his head but didn't speak. This was Eric's show.

"Luca is my uncle," Eric informed the old man.

"Why didn't your mother come here herself?"

"She's dead. So is my father."

Sullivan took a minute to think that over. His next comment hit Eric like a punch. "You're not coming here to live. I don't care how much money you have. My wife, Sylvia, doesn't like kids. I can't say I'm crazy about them either."

"Obviously," Eric snapped. "You left my mother at the age of five and never looked back. Do you have any idea what that did to her?"

Sullivan looked away. "That's not my problem, kid. I had good reason to leave your grandmother. I couldn't show my face in Jacksonville for years."

"You're right about that. It was my problem. It was a problem for everyone who loved my mother. She was a broken woman who lived in a pit of despair, never feeling loved, because of you."

Sullivan eyed Eric with an expression of hate. "Why are you here, kid?"

"I'm here to tell you, you're a disgusting slug. You don't have any idea what it is to be a man. I can see why my grandmother turned to someone else."

"If your mother was anything like her, you should question your own paternity."

Eric knew that was meant to be a low blow. Even though there was doubt about who his father actually was, he realized it didn't matter. But he wasn't finished with this worm yet. "I don't care about paternity. I know what it takes to be a father. It takes someone willing to see his family through hard times as well as good. It takes a man who's dedicated to standing up for the people who count on him. It takes someone who'll spend time teaching, guiding, encouraging, even if that thing is just understanding his homework or how to sink a ball through the net. It takes being there."

"I suppose you think I should have raised that bastard your grandmother gave birth to."

Eric glared back at his grandfather. "I'm glad you didn't. You would have broken her, too. She was all my mother had to make her life bearable after the punishment you put her through. She's a better woman than your trophy wife will ever be and more than you deserve."

Sullivan stomped toward the door. "I think you should leave and never darken my door again."

Eric smiled. "I certainly don't intend to stay, but let me leave you with one last thought. The day will come when I'll have the chance to ruin you."

Luca stood and nodded to Sullivan with a smile. They walked out without another word.

In the elevator, Luca shoved Eric's shoulder. "You were a friggin' beast in there."

Eric laughed. He felt like he could fly.

Chapter Thirty-Four

Monday, October 15—The Final Decision

Judge Alexander Benedict looked out from his bench to see that only one table was occupied before him. Joy Sullivan and Luca Wolff sat with Eric Wolff between them. He wished he could make his decision for two guardians, but the law was the law.

The seats behind them weren't empty this time. Gerald Wolff sat at one end of the first row. Three others, a woman and two men, sat at the other end. There wasn't an attorney in sight. It was just as well. He'd given the situation a lot of thought and made up his mind. "I've kept abreast of everything that has occurred over the last two months. You people have been through more than I could have predicted. Therefore, I'll overlook the fact that you didn't stay in the same house the entire time. From what I've been told you did stay in constant contact. And, although I never like to see a family torn apart, I'm glad the drama has come to an end.

"After our last meeting, I went back over both wills. I've decided the wills will stand as written. I ordered attorney Michael Knight to send me checks for each of you."

The bailiff collected two envelopes from the judge

and handed Luca and Joy each one.

The judge folded his hands and resumed addressing them all. "Now, regarding Eric. I hope he will continue a good relationship with you both. According to Dr. Johnson, that is his desire. Eric will no longer be required to attend sessions with the doctor. However, Dr. Johnson has asked me to pass the message that his door is always open if needed. That includes all of you.

"Eric will no longer have a caseworker. However, Mr. Meyers has offered a friendly ear if his advice would be useful. He's calling Eric his greatest success story.

"It is also decided that regardless of DNA, David Wolff's name is listed as the father on Eric's birth certificate. Also, David and Melissa Wolff were legally married at the time of his birth. Therefore, Eric will inherit as David's will states with Luca Wolff as the executor."

The judge took a deep breath and studied the anxiety on each person's face but directed his gaze at Luca. "Mr. Wolff, have you learned anything by this experience?"

Luca stood. "Yes, Your Honor. This co-parent project, as you called it, has been a humbling experience. It's caused me to have a different view of the world outside my own environment. It's also given me a different perspective of what makes a family. I'll always cherish the things I've learned from Joy and Eric."

"I'm glad to hear it. Do you have anything to say, Miss Sullivan?"

She stood as Luca took his seat. "Yes, sir. I agree with Luca, but the experience has been more empowering for me. I believe it has given me the tools to make a better life for myself as well as Eric. We've been through a lot together—all three of us. We've made a good team."

The judge turned to Eric. "What do you have to say about all that?"

"We are a team, Judge-Your Honor-Sir. They've taught me both those things. I'm humbler than I was and more empowered. I'm embarrassed by my past behavior and intend to stay on a good path. I need both these guys. We're a family."

"I appreciate what you're saying, son. And that makes the next part of this harder. I can only name one of them as your guardian. It was one of the toughest decisions I've ever had to make."

"Mister Luca Wolff, you brought the discrepancy of Eric's DNA to the attention of the court. I understand that your motivation was to, let's say, cut your brother's case out from under him. However, it's the reason I've decided to give Miss Sullivan guardianship.

"Does anyone have any questions?"

"I have something to say, Your Honor." Luca stood. "Throughout my adulthood, I've discovered that DNA has very little to do with what makes a family. A name means nothing until it's etched into your heart. Eric and Joy will both always be part of me, part of my heart, my family. I'd love to have Eric with me, but there's no one I'd trust more with his care than Joy. Don't feel bad about this. We're going to be just fine."

****

Luca couldn't deny his sense of disappointment, but he'd meant every word he'd said. Eric was beside the bench to shake the judge's hand and have a word with him. Joy was talking to the rest of the family. They were firming up plans for the end-of-court celebration tonight.

His father walked toward him with a sad expression on his face. He shook Luca's hand. "I'm sorry you lost, son."

"I haven't lost yet, Dad. Joy is fantastic with Eric. She's an amazing woman. If all goes well, I'll get them both back. I intend to marry her."

"I wish you luck then." After a pat on the back, the old man went over to talk to Eric.

Nelson said from behind him. "If you'd said something, this would have ended differently."

"It's not over yet." Luca turned to face his old friend. "I'm happy for Joy. She deserves this. I intend to ask her to be my wife. Not because of Eric, but because I can't live without her. I don't want her decision to be based on the threat of losing Eric. I want to know that she loves me too. Then, I'll find a way to tell them both the truth."

"It sounds risky to me, sir."

"What is life without a little risk?"

****

When Luca walked out of the courtroom, Joy rushed to catch up to him. "I'd never try to come between you and Eric. You know that, don't you?"

Luca smiled down at her. "It's still nice to hear you say it. So, are you ready to open that new salon? You know it's still sitting there waiting for you."

"You mean, you're still willing to back me on that?"

Luca gave her a curious look. "If you're still willing to take me on as a partner. You don't need me as a backer anymore."

"What do you mean?"

It took a moment for Luca to answer. "You haven't opened the envelope yet. I admire your decorum. Move back in with me. It'll be so much easier as our relationship heats up. I expect it to reach the boiling point by tonight."

Joy looked all around to see who may be listening. "You're outrageous! I have my own house."

"We can sell it. Better yet, we'll rent it to Arnold and Dinah. They're looking for a bigger place. Hell, we'll give it to them. Say you'll move back in. I miss you. Do you remember me telling you how a person's experiences make them who they are—and shared experiences make people closer? We've shared so much in the last couple months."

Joy shook her head. "Those are just memories that will diminish as new experiences come along."

Luca took her hands. "If we stay together, that can't happen. I want to share everything with you from now on—you and Eric—and any other little Wolffs that come along."

Joy laughed. "It sounds like you're planning to form a whole Wolff pack."

"We'll start with the three of us and see what happens."

Luca was moving in for a kiss when Eric ran up to join them. "Is anybody else hungry?"

Luca gave Joy a sexy wink. "You have no idea how hungry I am."

A word about the author...

From childhood I've moved from place to place, from Indiana to Florida, stopping in several places in between. I also moved from job to job, as a waitress, soldier, retail manager, dental assistant, etc. The one thing I never had to leave behind was my imagination.

Storytelling has always been my favorite way to pass time. I've often been told I should write a book. Finally, I did. It was so much fun: I feel I must write more, so I have.

I've been a student of Long Ridge Writers Group and once won a short story contest with Harlequin.

I currently live in north Florida with my husband, whom I torture with crazy story lines and half-written manuscripts.